STARVING ZOE

C. DERICK MILLER

DEATH'S HEAD PRESS
an imprint of Dead Sky Publishing, LLC
Miami Beach, Florida
www.deadskypublishing.com

ISBN: 978-1-63951-042-9

First Edition

Cover Art: Justin T. Coons

The "Splatter Western" logo designed
by K. Trap Jones

Book Layout: Lori Michelle
www.TheAuthorsAlley.com

For my wife Sam.
With you, all things are possible.

For our cat Zoe.
Meow.

I read Edward Lee, Hunter S. Thompson, and J. D. Salinger in the same week. This is the result.

CHAPTER ONE
Until Now . . .

FORGIVE ME IF I begin to ramble. I've been known to do that during times of high stress, otherwise known as my day to day life. Also, forgive any parts of my vocabulary which makes you scratch your head in confusion. The misfortunes of my many travels have placed me into circles of speech unlike those of the most common folk who barely traverse past their own front door. To put it plainly, I talk funny sometimes.

Someone once told me you can never go home again. Men say a lot of nonsense when they're facing death, mostly because they're scared as hell. You never know when the next bullet fired will have your name on it. At least the guy who told me those words of wisdom didn't. Poor bastard. You can never go home. I'd put that in a book for him if I could write worth a damn. Read? Sure. I read every chance I got. Write? Never. Perhaps someone else will do it.

Writer types, I swear. I was stuck in a damn trench with that guy and all his words of wisdom. Longest month of my life. Get this, he was from New York. New goddamn York! All the man ever talked about was writing a story where a soldier went astray and wandered around Manhattan for a weekend. What was so damn special about Manhattan? Been there before. Not impressed. When I asked him why he wasn't fighting for the other side, he just kept repeating that the Union soldiers were all a bunch of fawneys. I remembered that word from growing up a street urchin and needed no explanation. I tell you; it was the longest month of my life. Now, I'm stuck in the middle of the second longest month of my life riding through this God forsaken desert on a horse named Poon.

This damned horse.

Of all the dumb animals I could've purchased at the last minute, I had to go and buy this creature. Poon? He came with that name. I would've named a horse something like Trigger or Lightning or Quick Shot. No, sir. I paid one hundred dollars for this four-legged abomination. Bought him from an Australian slave trader on the banks of the Mississippi who was trying anything he could to persuade some of the freed blacks to 'work' for him on the boat back across the ocean. Some of those poor souls were falling for it but who am I to keep someone from learning a hard lesson in trickery? Those who were dumb enough to sign the unread contracts would figure it out sooner or later.

I never cared for those silly Australians anyway. I should've known from the beginning of the conversation that one of them would get over on me the first chance he got. I never would've guessed it would be with a horse, though. I've always been smart when it came to those things. Animals, I mean. This one? There was no fixing what he had wrong unless you counted a gunshot between his crossed eyes. I've been on his back now for weeks and still can't understand how he figures out where to go. The damn world must look like a swirled mess of greens and browns. When you're in front of him? Forget about it! All he does is stare at you like some lunatic who'd been dropped on their head one too many times at birth. You can lead a horse to water, but you can't stop him from slobbering in it. Drinks it right back up, he does. Makes me want to vomit every time I see him do it too. Slimy, thick spit full of boogers and whatnot sliding back down his throat. Idiot.

Now I'm stuck with him.

Even that name of his just makes me want to blow his equine brains all over this desert! Here, Poon! Come here, Poon! Can you imagine how damn stupid that sounds? If anyone was out in this wasteland who could hear me blabbering at that beast, they would probably go ahead and put me out of my misery in the same way I want to destroy this horse. I was two days into the ride before another Aussie informed me that 'Poon' was a slang term for "imbecile". Laughed and laughed as though I was supposed to know that. How in the hell was I supposed to know anything about the language some criminal spawn came up with around a campfire while sucking the bones of dead kangaroos? They just made it up! Right from scratch. Decided they didn't like normal speak and just threw in some random letters and some clicking sounds and that's what they came up with. Poon! So, here I am, riding through this unforgiving desert on the back of a loony horse named Poon. It's rubbish, I tell you.

Pure and simple rubbish! He'd be better off with no name at all. Just ride through this desert on a horse with no name. Poetic justice or the worst parts of my luck, I guess I'll never know. I've never been one for being a lucky soul since I inhaled the first breaths of this cruel world. Maybe you'd understand my story more if I took you all the way back to the beginning. Even further back than the tit sucking parts with me and my mother. Those particular bits are between she and I and none of your concern.

My name is Robert Jack. I've heard a million people say over the years that you can never trust a poor bastard who goes by two first names, but that's the one bestowed upon me. I can't even say what my hometown or village was because the two of them were killed dead in the street before I was even old enough to walk. Yes sir! Barely had my own two eyes open before they were dragged from their jail cells and butchered like animals at the hands of those slavers. Doesn't that sound like a hoot? There were white folks sold into slavery the same way the blacks were in Africa. Dragged kicking and screaming, they were. I can't rightly say that I know all the details because no one cared enough to write them down. The people at the orphanage only told me bits and pieces of it all before kicking me into the streets of Boston at age ten. It was better than nothing, I guess. Could've been a hell of a lot worse. Could've been Cleveland.

Rumor has it that my mother and father were some big figures in a local rebellion back in the North of my home country of Ireland. They didn't much care for the drivel going on around them, so they gathered up some like-minded folks and bashed in the brains of those who were attempting to dictate their lives. Sure, sweating your soul away on a potato farm isn't necessarily my idea of a good time, but doing it for the purpose of feeding some unknown government arseholes draws the lines between sweat and tears. They did what any other person would do when the time came to put a stop to things they didn't agree with. They rallied up the neighbors, grabbed the first sharpened tools they could get their hands on, and stuck them straight into the still beating hearts of those landlords. I guess they frowned upon that because my Ma and Pa were thrown into a dungeon awaiting trial and execution. In the meantime, there was me. Tiny little Robert Jack, all soiling himself and barely off those tits I was just talking about. I'm not even sure if that's really my damn name.

They stuck me on the boat to this God forsaken country before my parents' blood was even finished draining into the cracks between the cobblestones. No one even bothered to pass along any personal information, just put me on the floating nursery to the new world. Someone yelled the word "baby" amid the screaming of the boat's whistle and the fool who caught me thought they'd said 'Bobby'. It stuck with me all the way to Boston. Bobby this and Bobby that and Dammit, Bobby! There's only so many times I could hear that in my life before I decided to go by the proper version of my imaginary name. I became Robert to anyone else I met in the good old streets of Boston when I was ten years old, struggling to even feed myself. It wasn't long after that when I learned there was strength in numbers.

You see, I wasn't the only orphaned child who got dumped out into the streets as soon as he or she was old enough to skin a cat. Yep, sometimes that's what we had to do. Grab some stray kitty cat by its tail and hold on for dear life. Bash that cute, little head into the closest rock or onto the street and cook him up. Just break his head against whatever you found until you could hear the little kitty cat brains squelch out between the cracks you made. It sounds like a horrible way to live to those rich folks in the big cities who keep those evil animals as pets but, to us, it meant our bellies got full enough to live another day. God knows there were enough of them running around the homeless unfortunates, eating the faces of the dead and stealing any other morsels they were able to scrounge up. Damn cats, man. It was a love/hate relationship, I guess. Can you imagine being some high and mighty, petticoat wearing bitch who turned the corner at the wrong time just to see a gang of snot faced kids roasting a cat? It should've been enough to make her think twice about spreading her legs to a man and spitting out a child of her own. The horror of witnessing poor Junior Son-Of-A-Bitch gnawing the legs off Fluffy, painting the nursery in fresh blood and fur.

Of course, killing cats wasn't the only thing going on in the back alleys of Boston in those days. Ten years old or not, you had to watch each other's backs and make a name for yourself if you wanted to survive. I remember it like it was only yesterday. Then again, I remember a ton of shite like it was only yesterday and eventually all those memories become a week. Safe to say, I remember it like it was only last week. Some old man was beating the living hell out of one of my gang with some big stick he'd broken off a tree. Still had the goddam bark and leaves on it. Absolutely, he was bashing my street partner like it was his job, so I did the only thing that seemed natural in a situation such as that. I snuck up behind the old gent and found a mighty good-sized knife while going for his wallet. Stabbed him over and over and over again, I most certainly did. The suction of the blade as it tore in and out of the wound and the hot blood pouring over my chilled hand was enough to make me a happy child for a minute or two. The old man fell right onto his decaying knees, bringing him down to a level I was more comfortable with. Did I stop? No sir, I didn't. I commenced to stabbing that prick right in his neck. Cut him so many times, so deep, that his head came clean off and rolled down the street into the Boston harbor. Those who were there to see the whole thing happen said that I didn't just jack his knife and his wallet, I jacked his soul as well. Swore they saw it jump right out of his body through the gaping holes I left. They all began calling me "The Jacker" at that point and it frightened anyone who slept in my alley. Unfortunately, that old man was an important kind of somebody and the boys with badges came looking for me. I took my newly bestowed surname, shortened it to Jack, and hopped a ship down to New York before they could get their hands on me. A middle name wasn't all that important, so I just accepted it for what it was. Robert 'No Name' Jack.

The next few years flew by and I don't honestly have much recollection of anything worth remembering. Starvation will do that to you. I slept where I could, whether it be the basement of a sailor's tavern or underneath piles of garbage on the streets of Manhattan. Let me tell you, there's nothing like being woke up by a discarded diaper cloth to the face in a trash pile. Sometimes, the old bitch got so lucky, she'd land the baby stain right on top of your face like she was actually aiming for it. Absolutely! Whatever it was that baby had digested would take a trip right into the old nostrils and, the next thing you know, you're smelling baby excrement for days. I was willing to do just about anything to stay warm in the winters and dry when the rains came, though. Of course, it didn't take long for me to make a name for myself in every borough of that damn town as well. Some of my Boston brothers and sisters had decided to follow my lead into the new city and began to tell tales of The Great Irish Soul Jacker from up North. Soon, the crime bosses began throwing money my way to do the deeds too dirty for their own hands.

I became pretty well recognized in New York by the time I was the ripe old age of eighteen. I say 'ripe old age' because most street kids didn't last more than a few years in those days. They'd freeze to death in the snow or succumb to some other thief's rage long before adulthood. You might say I was one of the lucky ones, but luck had absolutely nothing to do with it. Pure skill, it was. The crime bosses and underworld kings tossed money at me like it was worthless to kill their adversaries and threaten anyone who opposed their dealings. Was it slavery? Yeah, I guess you could call it that. The only difference was . . . I was getting paid. I was being paid well, too. The other perk which came along with the whole package was fear. I was a killer for hire who rarely turned down a job. Women? Children? They were off the table completely. Inadvertently? Sure. I had no problem leading them to their death with booby traps and such, but I never put a hand on them. Murder by proxy, you could call it. The money men? Scared to death. After all, I knew where they slept, ate, and walked at all times. So, slavery? Certainly, but I was always the master.

Of course, 'The Jacker' sounded entirely too much like a nickname for a villain in a British murder novel and I began gaining attention by the men with the tin stars again. Some detective bastard had a bright idea in his sleep and started to pass around the notion that a serial killer or rapist may be on the loose. Not me, my good fellow. I wasn't into rape. I didn't have to be. There were tons of women on the streets of that city who would throw pussy my direction as though it was some type of store-bought treat meant for beasts of burden at a carnival petting zoo. The cops were just a bunch of lazy arsholes and generalizing for the ease of simple explanation. I had to tighten up my belt a bit to stay one step ahead of them. They never even came close.

It was humorous to watch them go from dive to dive, accusing any scum they came across of being the one and only Boston Jacker. Hell, most times I would just sit there, staring into my pint and trying not to burst into laughter at their tactics. It almost became a routine, really. Squatting in the Irish pubs, observing, as some poor dunce got his face bashed in on account of my actions. No one dared turn me over. Yes sir! Celebrated my young face like I was a hero to the boroughs or savior to those in need. There was even a time when I considered using my skills for good, but crime paid a hell of a lot better than playing Jesus Christ to the unfortunate. Sure, if I saw someone else harming a poor fellow for something they didn't deserve, I would step in. Now that I think about it, I bashed the faces in of many a fellow criminal just for squeezing into my territory. I could see where my neighbors would think it was done to benefit their safety, but they were dead wrong. Then again, they did keep me a secret from the police search parties constantly combing the neighborhoods. The double-edged sword of righteousness? Whatever makes you sleep easier at night and wake with all your limbs intact, I guess.

Before long, I began to see writing on the faded stone walls of Manhattan paying homage to the hero of the shadows. Almost laughed myself to death the first time I saw it. "God Bless The Jacker". What were these people thinking? Still, it kept me out of jail, so I was thankful for their delusions. Whatever kept the money and blood flowing was fine by me. Soon, I never paid for a meal, a shot of whiskey, or a shag. Royalty, I was. Criminal royalty in the streets of New York. Shortly after that, the women got a lot better looking as well. Beautiful things falling at my feet like I was king dick squirming down the alleys and between their legs into my kind of heaven. Sometimes it was even two or three at once. That was when I met Zoe Telos.

Zoe Telos. Man, let me tell you about that angel. Pure fire in a jar, she was. I shanked some sailor on shore leave who was trying to have his way with her and she started following me around like a stray dog. She was fourteen, I tell you. Four-damn-teen! Not in my neighborhood and not on my watch. The best thing about our meeting was when she jumped onto his gasping chest and stabbed him into the next life. That sailor looked like mush by the time she was done with him. All big puddles of blood with little canoes of skin following a trail through the cracks of the wooden docks. It's a nice gesture to feed the fish every now and then and they were loving every second. Splashing around underneath that dock every time a drop of blood hit the water. Old Zoe. Even though she didn't need it, I took her under my wing and schooled her in all things street. Before long, we were a team to be reckoned with and splitting the money fifty-fifty. When it was all said and done, I would snuggle that little sweetheart to sleep without laying a finger on or in her. On my honor, I swear. She was basically still a child, but I was so in love with her. In love enough to do the right thing. Can you believe it? I did the right thing. Never touched her inappropriately. There are just some hells you can't pull yourself out of, even as a couple of orphans on the streets of New York City.

Good old Zoe Telos was a scrounger and a hustler just like me and she'd been doing things that way since she was old enough to walk. Her mother was a Greek prostitute somewhere in Brooklyn who made the mistake of getting knocked up. Since her existence was a hinderance to her Mom's money maker, Zoe was turned out into the streets to fend for herself with another group of girls who weren't far off. Her companions were turning tricks left and right to stay alive, but she was way too young. As a man with any sense of ethics, I'd never look twice at some kid whose nether regions still smelled like pee no matter how cute they were. Unfortunately, there's a ton of guys strolling around this world who don't see things the way I do. I never asked, but I'm sure Zoe did her share of things she wasn't proud of to survive on those streets before she met me. It wasn't any of my business. My world seemed to exist in the here and now. She squirmed in her sleep a lot. Talked sometimes, too. Evil, evil men walking around in this world, let me tell you. No, kept her safe and sound in my arms and never made a move on her regardless of my feelings. No sir. I loved Zoe Telos with all my heart. Loved her enough to make me realize it was time to leave the mean streets of New York City for good.

You see, Zoe and I were in the process of assisting a neighborhood ghoul into the underworld when a badge turned the corner. Come to find out, people in the up and up neighborhoods considered this son of a bitch to be someone important, a judge or something along those lines. I honestly couldn't have cared less, and Zoe agreed to my logic wholeheartedly. We were out at the docks cutting off one finger at a time with a pair of secateurs and feeding them to the fish again. Those little bastards just love it when you pay them any type of special attention. It was typical Zoe at its finest! It was a pretty quiet night and you could hear the blades rip as she slowly invaded the man's flesh. Then, the snap of bone would echo through the fog and the bloke screamed like a banshee for anyone to come to his aid. After that, she'd dangle them over the water and tease the fish before finally giving them a treat. All I did was sit on the aging pervert to keep him from getting away. No sir, I barely even touched him. It was all Zoe. I loved her that much, I did. Then, someone finally came to help our latest victim. Yes sir, a damn copper turned the corner just as we finished with the left hand and was about to begin on his right. I stuck that cop right through his eye hole with an ice pick and gave his brain something to think about. Of course, this was after he'd given his warning rattle a good shake and I knew more of them would be bearing down on us soon. We had to disappear fast. Didn't even finish killing the deviant. Just let him bleed from his nubs on the dock still squirming.

We ran back to our room above Fannin's Tavern and gathered up as much money as our bags could hold. Didn't even bother to stash any extra clothing or personal belongings. We just packed money for our trip to anywhere, we did. Didn't even have the slightest idea where we were going but the two of us agreed it needed to be in a westerly direction. Lots of who's and what's were moving out West every damn day and it suddenly appeared as though we'd be two of them. Hopped the first train out of New York City headed West with bags full of spending cash and no clothes other than what we had on our two backs. Just me and my fourteen-year-old lover who I'd never laid a finger on or in for the sake of being no better than the ancient judge we'd just been using as bait. Zoe laid her child-like head on my shoulders out of pure exhaustion and uncertainty, and the two of us said goodbye to the cruel city of New York forever. Home awaited us on the frontier even though Zoe and I knew nothing of our final destination.

C. Derick Miller

A few train changes, a bumpy wagon ride, and a couple hundred dollars later, Zoe Telos opened her young eyes to the newly founded Arizona territory at the edge of the New West. Yes sir, accepted us with open arms, they did. Well, they accepted us after the yokels learned to decipher our speech. Most times, they would just stand there with their heads cocked to the side like confused dogs. The great American Civil War had begun and the Confederates, who'd claimed the Northern portion of the Arizona territory, were looking for any kind of friend they could find. Kicking out them Indians left and right and sending them east into New Mexico territory and beyond or slaving them out to fight the Yankees from back home, they were. It was nasty business, that slavery, no matter what the color of your skin was but it didn't make me and Zoe any never mind because, as far as an outsider's perspective went, we were just another two penniless orphans running from something. They rarely bothered us for that simple reason. You can't raise too much hell if you don't have the funds to pay for it, right? Me and Zoe Telos barely afforded a tent and some supplies from the nearest general store and made our home in the pine forests of the Northern Arizona Territory away from the eyes of the new world. A few days after that, I pulled out an axe and got to work on our forever home.

Before long, I'd made me and Zoe a place to be proud of. To be certain, I slightly overdid it just a bit, but there was nothing in this great wide world too good for my sweet Zoe Telos. Absolutely, made a second story to that house for our bedroom and any other spaces which might be needed in the coming

STARVING ZOE

years. You see, that sniveling kid I'd inadvertently fallen in love with on the mean streets of New York City had finally reached the ripe old age of seventeen, and I thought it only nice and proper to put a ring on her finger and seal the deal. She accepted without hesitation when I asked because I knew deep down that she'd felt the same way about me all these years. No sir, I wasn't about to be branded any kind of degenerate for no reason, no matter how many times she snuggled up against me in the night and asked for it. I made her my wife and gifted her the nicest house either of us had seen with our tainted eyes in all the Arizona Territory. We'd even discussed the possibility of beginning a family when the law came knocking, pitchforks and torches in hand like we were monsters in a Grimm's story. It seems that tales travel fast even though neither of us hadn't so much as lifted a knife to anyone's throat since exiting the train to our new lives. It also seems that unfinished jobs can travel great distances to come back and bite your tail at any time of the day or night.

Someone objected right in the middle of the ceremony. Have you ever heard of that before? Sure, you have in rumor, but have you ever heard of someone truly having the gumption to do that? My wedding day came to a screeching halt at the raise of a hand which looked all too familiar. All palm and five nubs. It seemed as though a certain fingerless judge was also trying to make a name for himself out in the great Wild West and happened to catch a mighty good glance at our faces during one too many trips into civilization. Yes sir! There was really no one there to put up much of a fight when he settled into the territory and set up shop as judge and executioner. We should've killed the man when we had the chance back in Yankee land. Our only loose end during our run as hired killers tracked us down and offered two simple options.

Option number one was simply out of the questions. It involved me and Zoe playing guest to his newly deputized marshals as they dragged the two of us kicking and screaming back to New York City to stand trial as murderers. What that loosely translated into was we'd be killed by his pistoleers somewhere between here and there and placed into shallow, unmarked graves. Now, I don't know this for sure but it's what I'd do to someone if given the chance on a miserable trip back east. Probably in Texas, I imagined. Of all the miserable places in the world to have coyotes kick the sand off you and make a meal of your unmentionables, Texas seemed like the only place where horrific situations like that could happen. There were some mean sons of bitches in Texas, let me tell you. Swiped that chunk of land straight out from under the Mexicans and stuck a flag in it as though they owned the place. Well, if you shoot enough people, it technically puts you in charge whether the locals like it or not, and those damn Texans were some trigger-happy cowboys. They'd shoot you right in the dick, they would, for no reason whatsoever. Never cross a Texan, and don't let them anywhere near your dick.

My only other option was to accept recruitment into the Confederate Army and fight the good fight of the Arizona Territory. The judge knew of my escapades in New York and even witnessed it himself

STARVING ZOE

before we split for the West. He seemed to think I could do his little militia some good if they were to ever get in a bind. With those two options laying at my feet it didn't seem like much of a choice at all, really. If I chose to serve the judge, at least the love of my life would be safe and sound in our home. Sure, she wouldn't have me there for protection, but Zoe didn't really need protecting. Without me in the territory, she officially became the meanest bitch in Arizona. Indians, bandits, wolves, rattlesnakes, and five fingered judges would need to sleep with one eye open from that moment on with my Zoe on the warpath. The biggest question beating around in my troubled mind was how in the hell I was going to survive every night without her by my side. On the other hand, how was she going to live out her day to day life without me in it? It was all scenarios we'd both have to work out because I refused for either of us to be residents of that shallow grave in Texas my overactive imagination had created. Yep, I was going to be a soldier for the boys in gray no matter how little I believed in their cause. At least the judge was kind enough to let us finish the ceremony.

A few days after that, I waved goodbye to my sweet Zoe, her Greek, black hair blowing in the desert breeze, and pointed my boots eastward. I was destined to do horrible things, but it was a small price to pay to get me back into the arms of the lady I loved. That, my friends, is how I got into my current predicament. Sure, there's tons more to it than what I've led you through, but we will get there eventually. Just have faith. I'm going to tell you the story of a friendship gone horribly wrong. Life on the streets taught me to always watch my back and never, under any circumstances, trust anyone. Ever. War taught me to always finish the job no matter the consequences . . . until now. What has life, in general, taught me up until this point in my tale? That's an easy answer. Forgiveness is overrated. Death is final. Revenge, however, dances between the fine lines of mortality and eternity. Love always finds a way. My name's Robert "The Jacker" Jack . . . and this is the honest telling of my story.

CHAPTER TWO

MONDAY

HOMECOMING

"**REALLY?**" **I SCREAMED** at my idiot horse as he halted yet again to drink from a small stream. "We are literally five miles away from my God forsaken house and you're stopping to drink again? I can see the lights in the windows from here!"

The poor, cross-eyed bastard looked back at me as though a single, rational thought failed to exist within his pea sized brain. Stupid animal. He'd done nothing but eat and spray feces since we crossed into the Arizona territory and I was sick of it. Sometimes he'd be doing both at the same time! How can you even do that? The smell of fresh dung wafting up your nose while you're chewing on grass? With a nose that big? Made me gag just thinking about it. All I wanted to do was get home. No sir, all he was interested in doing was licking any puddle of wetness his slanted vision picked up on and then drop a pile of the most foul-smelling waste imaginable in our wake. The beast was probably lapping up his own piss and didn't even know it. Goddamn Poon! Four years' absence from my sweet Zoe was long enough without having to deal with this equine manure machine on the edge of my own property. My left hand held tight to my right wrist, preventing me from reaching for my gun. I had no problem walking the rest of the way but, in the grand scheme of things, a man never knows when he'll need a fast getaway. A horse would be a handy tool in such situations. Any horse but this one.

I jest you not, I was attempting to make up for lost time a few nights ago when this four-legged science experiment of God gone horribly wrong slowed his run down to a near crawl. Suddenly, I heard a rustle in the underbrush below me and thought the dumb animal had somehow managed to trample through a nest of rattlesnakes. Then, he came to a complete stop. No longer hearing the disturbance in the brush, I jumped down from my saddle to see how to solve his newest quirk. The horse was galloping with a hard-on and somehow managed to get his dick jammed in between two rocks. I swear to Jesus on a stack of Bibles that's what happened! I didn't want to touch the veiny protrusion, so I began smacking it with the butt of my Colt pistol. Smacked that son of a bitch so hard I thought it would break in half. No sir, that's not what happened at all! Old Poon commenced to shaking and shimmying like he was on the verge of having the mother of all seizures. Then, splat! The four-legged abomination let go a wad of horse shot all over the rocks and I jumped backward like I'd just discovered a stack of explosives! Before too long, his ugly stick slithered back up inside its sheath and he continued to trot again. Idiot just started walking like nothing ever happened. I wasn't even on his back! Would've shot him dead in his tracks if I wasn't in such a hurry to make it home. There's a special place in Hell reserved for this horse but I refuse to be the one who sends him there. All I wanted to do was climb into bed next to Zoe Telos Jack. Nothing was going to stop me, not even this horny, piss drinking, cross-eyed horse.

Dozens of war driven nightmares came flooding into my head the second I crossed the boundary into what I hoped was still my own land. I hadn't received any letters from Zoe for nearly a year now. My head swam with the possibilities. Dangerous waters, the ones in your own head. Worse than any which exist in the real world. All of them full of gators and snakes and dark as mud. They stir up all the bad thoughts no one wants to think about. No one with half a brain, anyway. No, Zoe was quite the correspondent for the first few years of my absence. Always sure to tell me everything going on in the Northern Arizona Territory that I'd missed. The one-handed judge didn't live too much longer after my departure, but she never explained one way or the other if it was her own handiwork. Didn't want the Pony Express to get bored on one of their long rides and turn up looking for any reward money being offered.

Hell, the government was still hesitant to bring the land into statehood for all the rogue Indians running loose. They were marching and shipping them by train into New Mexico and Oklahoma as fast as they could, but it just wasn't quick enough. In her last letter, Zoe even wrote that she'd made friends with a family of Indians and was trading their protection for a little spot in the pines to stay safe from the troops. That's what worried me the most. Sure, the red skins were protecting my wife from the wildlife and bandits, but who was protecting her from the Indians? Something told me I'd run into some of them soon enough, and it wasn't going to be a pleasant meeting either. Not that I had anything against them personally, but the color of someone's skin wouldn't stop me from putting the whoop on the ones responsible for breaking up my happy home. That home was all that kept me going over the last few years and it would take a bad son of a bitch to snatch it out from under my wayward feet.

I led Poon through the shallows of the Verde River and damn near fell off the son of a bitch in amazement. He didn't even attempt to lower his head into the cool, flowing water for a taste. The idiot had no problem whatsoever slurping up his own salty piss, but the clean water from that river was completely off limits. Crazy, I tell you. Either his parents were overbred to the point of insanity or his previous owner beat him about his head until pure stupidity took hold for good. Goddamn Poon!

The midnight moon was dangling high in the sky when I crept up the wrap around porch to my own front door. I couldn't help but utilize all the perks the surrounding forest had to offer when I built our little love nest. No, sir. Anything my sweet Zoe wanted, she got. I didn't care how long it took. I'd planned on making her every dream come true the second I picked up that hammer for the first time. My blood, sweat, and tears stained the wood of that porch, and if you looked closely enough in the broad daylight, you could see exactly what I was talking about. Little droplets of my hard work became a part of this place with every swing of that damned hammer and curse word uttered. I eased off my dusty boots as stealthily as possible and placed my hole-covered socks on the frigid lumber. A sigh of relief the likes of which I didn't think possible exited my smiling mouth and alerted Poon. He jerked his head up hard against the secured reins and damn near pulled the hitching post from the ground. Maybe if I repeated the process a few times he would break his own neck. At least I wouldn't have to live with the guilt of killing him myself.

"Keep quiet, stupid!" I shushed the poor beast but all he could do was stare at me blankly with his cross-eyed gaze. Somewhere on my gun belt was a bullet with his name on it, but not tonight. A gunshot in the darkness was a sure way to get my sweet Zoe Telos out of bed and probably get me shot as well. She was never one to hesitate on the trigger of that rifle. To boot, my bride hadn't the slightest idea I was coming home. Absolutely! She'd put a hole right between my own two eyes making me look no better than that Poon horse! I was going to sit there on that porch and contemplate the best course of action when it came to her finding out her husband was home for good. I just hoped the war hadn't spoiled my good looks any. There weren't too many mirrors between my home and the front lines and, for all I knew, I currently resembled some type of rabid beast.

My creaking, war beaten bones cracked as I got to my feet. The glow from a half-extinguished fire filled the main room, throwing unrecognizable shadows in all directions against the walls. I jumped slightly but gained my composure with a quiet giggle. Things like that used to make my skin crawl back in the day, but I'd become a full-fledged, Yankee charging son of a bitch since then. It took a hell of a lot more than some creepy light trickery to get my goose going nowadays. I finished my sudden shiver and began to ascend the stairway in the direction of our upstairs bedroom. I was so damn close; I could almost feel the softness of my old bed wrap around my exhausted body. None of that would matter, though. Four long years of abstinence plagued my heart and cock and it was about damn time I did something about it. Let me tell you, there was a ton of fine-looking women in the Southern states just aching to feel a Confederate soldier blast one between their legs, but I was as pure as a man could be when it came to such things. I'd promise on a stack of a million Bibles, I would. Never did I ever. These pants stayed on my body until nature called and for no other reason. It was my Zoe or nothing else, I tell you. I'd made that promise to God right before that one-handed judge came half knocking and I meant every word of it. Handling that situation any other way could sneak back up on a man somewhere down the road and cause all kinds of evil. That wasn't me. Not anymore. I didn't believe in cheating. Cards or crotch. What's mine was mine.

Finally reaching the top of the stairway, I could hear the sweet inhale of Zoe's snore fill the bedroom like a long, lost treat. I'd always found it cute instead of annoying, unlike most couples when they stay together for longer than they should and begin hating on each other. No sir, it was nothing but cute in my book. Always liked it. When you were still asleep, in that state of mind just before waking and you can hear things, that sweet little snore was always there to let me know that the love of my life was alive, well, and waiting for me. Honestly, I didn't know how much longer I could wait to be there. It took everything I had not to shuck my dusty clothes to the floor and jump onto that bed. Absolutely, just jump right smack dab in the middle of those beautiful tits and kiss those lips like there'd be no tomorrow. My dick heard me thinking and jumped to attention like a parade soldier half asleep and realizing it was his turn to salute. Now wasn't the time, though, because I'm sure she'd want to hear a little more explaining on my part rather than my road beaten cock swinging all over the place. I tucked the thing back down my pants leg and prayed for some quick relief with every step. That was when I heard it.

As soon as the blood ran out of my dick and back into the vicinity of my ears, I began to realize my Zoe wasn't the only person snoring in that bedroom of mine. My back hair stood on edge like an enraged dog as I scanned the dimly lit room for the unfortunate soul who'd entered the wrong house on this special night. Old Zoe was sure enough in bed alone, I was damn sure of it, because I only witnessed a single lump between the blankets. Not that I'd ever wondered for a single second that she'd been unfaithful to me in my absence, but a man has got to make sure, doesn't he? After all, I'd been gone for four damn years and women tend to do funny things when they get all lonely. Sure, they can get off by sticking a finger or two down inside their coot or whittle off a tree limb in the shape of a cock to make it all happen for them, but I guess the feel of the real thing is always next to perfect. That's a good way to get a termite infestation up in your puss, fucking a tree and all. I wouldn't go around recommending it for anyone who was a big fan of hygiene. No sir, for a fraction of a second, I thought I'd be able to forgive her if I'd seen her all snuggled up next to some strange man after me being gone for so long. Then, good sense came back to visit. My second thought assured me I would've killed the son of a bitch before tucking back into that pussy. She was all alone in that bed and still mine all mine. Then my eyes finally adjusted to the darkness of my bedroom to reveal the culprit responsible for the second set of breaths. The baby crib in the corner was the only hint I needed to deliver my playing piece to the next square of the game. My heart sank somewhere into the vicinity of my worn out feet and showed no signs of returning soon. My world disappeared into a sea of red.

I could no longer be responsible for the actions of Robert Jack. No sir, he was beyond the capacity of rational thought as he tiptoed across the hard wood floor to take a gander at the sleeping little demon. Now, I know I'm talking as though I was outside of my own body watching it all play out from a distance, but that's exactly what it felt like. I couldn't stop myself no matter how hard I tried. I didn't care for explanations or excuses. They'd come, but I didn't care. I'd heard Zoe fib her way out of numerous serious situations over our years together. I'd be damned if I was going to let her play me for a fool. I was born at night but it sure wasn't last night! I was officially a poker player in a fifty-two-card pickup kind of world, and this slumbering abomination was my royal flush. See what I mean? All kinds of nonsense running through my pain-pinged brain. I was at the mercy of my own creation. The Jacker, war-torn and all grown up, had come back for a visit. As of right that second, he was smiling ear to ear as he cradled the tiny, unconscious infant in his arms. This wasn't going to end well at all.

The baby was a deep red in color which led me to believe Zoe had banged around with those Indians one too many times in my absence. It hurt me so much to even think about it. My arms felt numb against the child's warm blankets. Just then, a tear streaked down my right cheek to land somewhere atop the floor, mixed with millions more from what felt like a lifetime ago. Back when I first built this place. Back when Zoe Telos loved me unconditionally. Those days were officially gone. No sir, there'd be no way back from this.

Silently as I could, I snuck back down the stairway and through the front door of my home to bathe the child in the blinding, desert moonlight. My heightened eyesight revealed the little devil to be quite an ugly son of a bitch as far as the looks of infants go. Sure, they're all sweeter than penny candy when they first get squeezed out the coot, but this abomination looked as though it'd been carried to the top of the ugly tree, dropped, and then hit its chin on every branch all the way down. Hit 'her' chin, actually. Sure enough, that little demon currently cuddled in my shaking arms was most definitely a little girl. That meant absolutely nothing as far as my alter ego was concerned. That little meat sack was probably dreaming all kinds of sweet things in that tiny little head. The girl didn't have the slightest idea she was taking the last few breaths among her fellow living souls upon the face of this messed up world. Not to worry, I thought to myself, this little bitch wasn't going to be the only death which came tonight, but she was sure as fucked fire going to be the first! I didn't even know the little whore's name. I didn't care to know. It was better that way.

My feet came to a halt at the foot of the water well long before I even realized I'd been walking that direction. Looking over my tired shoulders, I realized the footprints through the sandy soil hadn't faltered not one bit as they'd made their way to what was certain to be this child's final place of rest. Just to add a bit of humor to the whole ordeal, I thumped the Satan spawn on her hideous nose so she could witness one final act of this life's cruelty before blinking out forever. The child's innocent eyes opened to the bright, celestial moon but soon returned to blackness as I released the burden into the confines of the well. I tipped my hat in farewell to the first of many horrific activities doomed to transpire on this night of my homecoming. The expected splash never came. I was only temporarily disappointed.

The faint thump of her landing echoed throughout the emptiness of the dry chasm. It must've been a dry summer in the Northern Arizona Territory because there wasn't a single drop of water in that well. Just then, my grin returned even wider as a symphony of rattlesnakes initiated their song of inevitability. Although I couldn't begin to imagine how they'd ever get their mouths around the meal I'd unexpectedly offered them during their unfortunate, eternal confinement, I was certain the venom would come. Tiny whimpers traveled to my waiting ears as the serpents struck the child repeatedly . . . and all was quiet once more. I could imagine those needle fangs tearing deep into the flesh of that poor, defenseless infant and the confusing thoughts that followed. How in the hell could something so evil penetrate the wholesomeness of a presumed innocent, tiny child? It was no longer my problem. Nature would have its way in the bottom of that well on this night. My mind swam with the horrors playing out dozens of feet below my blood-stained soles, and I couldn't care less about any of it. Not my child, not my problem. Feed the snakes, young one. Feed them.

The current state of my dead brain somehow instructed my feet to turn toward the house one more time to finish the deeds I'd concocted out of sinister, yet silent rage. The Jacker wasn't quite sure how he planned on bringing the festivities to a screeching halt. The one sure thing battling for supremacy in his mind was how he intended on making it last until the morning sun peered above the Arizona horizon. Yes sir, old Zoe Telos and I were going to get very reacquainted over the next few hours. Trust me, the things she'd witnessed since the early days of our coming together were forgettable, even unimpressive, when compared to what the soldier in me had been forced to do in the face of my Union enemies. Feelings of remorse no longer existed after the first two or three bashed faces. If the blood of the fallen truly fed the foliage of this planet, then everywhere I'd visited over the last few years was covered in the brightest green imaginable. The only question which remained was how I planned to keep the coming scenario fun and enjoyable while teaching my Zoe the last great lesson she'd ever need to learn.

I made it all the way back up into my tainted bedroom with the stealth of a house cat. Of course, all the silence in the world couldn't keep those knees of mine from cracking and popping like someone had taken a gun belt full of bullets and thrown it into a campfire. Lots of miles on those ancient knees and they just couldn't help it. At first, I reached for Zoe's mouth when she stirred but I knew damn well no one would hear her scream if that was where she planned on taking it. No sir, it wasn't like she was going to wake the baby or anything along those lines. I'd taken care of that little issue long before Zoe's eyes adjusted to the darkness. I spoke first to assure the conversation was headed in the direction I saw fit.

"Where's your red man?" I whispered. Now, in most situations, this would be where the woman tried to lie her way out of the situation, all squirming and pleading, but my girl knew better. I'd slipped the cold steel of my Colt underneath those warm blankets and right off into her coot, cocked and ready. She didn't even flinch. Damn Red Man had gone and messed up my fit five minutes after I'd kissed her goodbye all those years ago. My brain was sure of it. The seconds ticked by like minutes before Zoe uttered her reply, but I knew it to be truthful. She wouldn't dare lie to me with a gun tucked deep in her puss. She knew better. Not that I'd ever tried something like this before on anyone, but it didn't take some school trained Yankee to figure out this was a serious situation. I was certain Zoe recognized that instantly.

"Been gone six months," she finally spoke. "He brought too much attention to himself. Hiding his people from the soldiers and leading raids on the supply wagons. They shot him dead to make an example to anyone else who'd get the idea of being a rebel between here and Gallup. Just me, little Jackie, and the Medicine Woman now."

Little Jackie? The cheating whore had the nerve to give that kid my made-up surname after she'd been pleasing Indians left and right? I couldn't help but laugh a bit at Zoe's misfortune. "No, darling, it's just the two of us now. I ain't seen no Medicine Woman and the baby took a tumble I don't think she'll recover from any time soon. Probably never. As a matter of fact, I'd be impressed if the little bitch isn't long dead already."

I could see the tears begin to streak down Zoe's face in the moonlight as it poured through the bedroom window. Not once did she ever shiver or try to remove the barrel of the gun I'd stuck up in her. Finality at its finest, for sure. Little Jackie? Was she serious? Banging around with those red devils and had the nerve to name his spawn after me? I had to shake that off, for sure. By no means was I anywhere near done with Zoe and I fought the urge to pull the trigger. That was about the time she spat out an obvious realization.

"Robert, I thought you were dead," Zoe whined. "The mail stopped coming over a year ago and I thought you'd been shot to pieces. I did what I had to do to survive. Weren't no way I was going to make it on my own out here and you know it!"

"Don't even begin to tell me what I know and what I don't know, you whore!" I replied without hesitation. "Even if you did think I was dead and buried, it didn't appear as though you gave it much thought before you began spreading your legs to the Indians and probably a few of those rogue Confederate soldiers too. At least you could've had the decency to keep it within the same color palette, Zoe! You had to go off and take a shot in the coot from one of those damned Indians? Savage bastards had to go and knock up my sweet Zoe! I swear, it makes me feel kind of sad to be shoving this gun up in there knowing how disgusted it must feel, just swimming around with all that Indian stew."

I paused with that thought. My outburst was one hundred percent correct and I pulled the barrel of my Colt out of her puss with a smack. The aiming sight at the end of the barrel must've snagged her little pleasure spot because I finally got that shiver from her I was looking for. I bet you it sure as hell wasn't from any kind of pleasure. No sir, that revolver of mine deserved so much better than to be shoved up inside the crack of some frontier Indian whore. No sooner than I'd rode away to war had this bitch put a sign on my front door welcoming in all the vagrants and red skins to come inside and get a piece. I was damn sure of it. Then again, it wasn't like anything Zoe had to say would've made any sense to me since the voice of The Devil himself had taken over. I pulled back the hammer on my Colt Army and contemplated the next move.

"Robert, don't you dare go killing me in this house or you're going to be in a world of hurt," my Zoe threatened. "The Medicine Woman is a real thing. I didn't just make her up to frighten you. If she's not here, then she's at least on her way back. If she finds me dead, she'll come after you. Guaranteed. She's probably coming after you anyway for killing her granddaughter. I'd get to walking, if I were you. Get as far away from this house as you can."

Old Zoe was getting good and desperate now trying to scare me with some Indian mumbo jumbo, but I wasn't about to fall for it. Yes sir, I'd seen many Union soldiers beg and plead for mercy, spouting all kinds of senseless babble on their mud-caked knees, trying to prevent me from painting the woods with their blood. None of that ever seemed to work for them. Turned the whole place from green to red on many instances no matter what kind of yarn they were trying to spin. Didn't benefit a damn one of them, and I wasn't about to start slipping on this night. Then again, my Zoe did make some sense when it came to how I'd end it all. Sure enough, killing was indeed too good for the love of my life. I pulled the trigger to send one of her kneecaps flying to the far corner of the bedroom. I grinned again as it smacked against the wall with a moist impact of blood on timber followed by the dull knock of the bone as it landed. She held onto the wound for dear life, but it didn't do her much good. In the end, I didn't need her to walk, I just needed to make sure she couldn't get away.

"Now hush, my darling Zoe," I whispered with false comfort. "We wouldn't want to wake up the imaginary Medicine Woman who sleeps downstairs, would we? I don't think you've taken our little conversation seriously up to this point, so it was about time I kicked it up to the next level. You do know I'm serious, right?"

Zoe nodded as her head convulsed side to side on the blood-stained pillow. Yes sir, I'd done exactly what I said I would do. You can't call Robert Jack a liar. Not once. I tucked the still smoking barrel of the gun deep into the wound, twisting and digging as though some kind of hidden treasure remained inside just hoping to be discovered. The aiming sight acted like a dull doctor's scalpel, roughly slicing the tormented flesh within. Zoe screamed in agony, clutching onto the ghost of her knee as I ripped the barrel free once more. Hell, it only seemed right to make the other one match. Her shriek of terror came to life once more as I pulled the trigger. That was about the time when I tossed my wailing, bleeding bride across my shoulders to make my way down the stairs and into the night. Hell, Poon didn't even acknowledge my presence as I reached deep into my saddle bag to retrieve rope. He'd inadvertently moved up the food chain on my list of things I loved since Zoe had taken a dive during the last hour.

"Wave goodbye to little Jackie," I taunted as we passed the barren well which had become a grave marker for Zoe's Navajo spawn. "I don't think the little bitch can hear you, being tucked off into the belly of a rattler and all, but you could damn sure try. No worries if you can't, though. I'll be sending you to the same Hell in a matter of minutes, Zoe Telos. Don't you worry your pretty little head about that. Your whole damned family will be reunited before the sun rises."

Zoe had finally stopped her kicking and wailing

somewhere between the house and the banks of the Verde River. Yes sir, I didn't see it fit for a man to kill his own wife, so I'd planned on letting nature take her the rest of the way. I slammed her near lifeless body against the protruding thorns of a Mesquite tree to make sure she'd go nowhere fast. I could see the sharpened points of the thorns which didn't quite make it through her skin as they poked the muscle from inside her useless arms. I went ahead and added a bit of rope to the enigma just to make sure Zoe didn't hit a noble streak and wander off in the direction of help. No sir, that wasn't my plan at all. A pack of animals, wolves or coyotes, would eventually come to the banks of the rushing Verde to quench their thirst. Lucky for them on this night, they'd find a fresh meal waiting, tied to this here Mesquite tree, and finish Zoe off good and proper. Till death do us part was only a good hour or so away, if all the blood didn't run out of her knees before then, and I would've withheld the hands of the killer in me from finishing the job. Not that I'd planned on going to heaven anytime soon, or even at all, but I didn't need this kind of a tarnished mark against my record when God Almighty came to call roll. I'm sure I'd be requesting help from the man upstairs soon enough. There must be a special place in Hell for cheating wives like Zoe Telos, and I just wanted to make sure she got where she was supposed to go. Washing my hands clean in the cold waters of the Verde, I glanced upon her frail figure one last time. If the wildlife didn't get to her, the elements surely would. Until then, I just had to ignore the cries of my sweet, starving Zoe.

CHAPTER THREE
TUESDAY
HOMESTEAD HORROR

THE CREAKING RHYTHM of my rocking chair sang a song of sadness atop the wraparound porch of the homestead. I'd had wet dreams of this chair almost as many times as I'd had them of my wife while I was away at war. Almost embarrassing to wake up with a raging stiff and your underclothes soaked with man gravy because of an inanimate object. I'll claim it, though. Any damn day. I loved this chair and it loved me back. Not once did it fuck an Indian while I was gone. I was sure of it.

My mind flipped through still images of old Zoe and I in all the years we'd been acquainted. Lots of things worth remembering as far as that pain-struck heart of mine was concerned. I lingered on a few of them here and there, but none as long as the view of her on our wedding day. Yes sir, right before that one-handed judge busted down the door, I was looking on a personal slice of heaven. Mine all mine until the red man came knocking on that puss of hers. Tears and smiles battled for supremacy on this hardened face and I wasn't quite sure how much longer I'd be able to hold back a good cry. That was right about the time this ancient Indian bitch Zoe'd been talking about placed her dirty feet atop my welcome mat.

"You're too late, witch," I barked nonchalantly. "I've already taken Zoe's cheating arse to the gates of Hell and, unless you're looking to make it admission for two, I'd start scooting those mangy feet of yours in the opposite direction."

I clicked back the hammer on the Colt Army just to make sure the point was driven home. I was half-expecting the crone to break down in tears, but she didn't even flinch! Scary bitch. I swear, I didn't think I'd ever be able to understand those damn home wrecking savages, and this old fart wasn't helping the process too much. No sir, she just stood there, and stared straight ahead at my front door like some invisible stranger was putting on a shadow puppet presentation against the moon. Wasn't nothing much more than a couple of moths fucking. Nothing worth watching in my mind. Damn bitch just kept on staring like it was the greatest show on Earth. Finally, her crusty lips parted to utter three small words.

"And the child?" she asked.

It took everything I had to hold back a laugh at her expense. I was getting better at doing such things. There was a time when I would burst out laughing in the face of someone who was trying to taunt me like I couldn't help it. Like I was a stupid kid whose best parts had dribbled down the crack of his mother's back side during conception. No sir, not at all. I didn't laugh in response to this idiot Indian woman's question in the slightest. I just stared straight ahead into the darkness of the desert the same way she was getting her happy juices flowing by watching the moths fuck. Those moths had some stamina, let me tell you! It was so quiet you could almost hear that little bug cock flopping in and out of her coot while the male was slamming her bug butt against the lantern glass. That is pretty quiet. One hundred percent! You know something horrible is about to go down when you can hear the moths fucking.

"Oh yeah," I replied, "Almost forgot about that little abomination. You'd better make that admission for three."

That will really cook her goose, I thought. Sure enough, if that don't chap her hide, nothing will. That's all I wanted out of her, really. Just a tad bit of emotion on the face of that walking statue wasn't too much to ask. After all, I'd thrown her granddaughter down a dry well full of rattlesnakes and then crucified her bitch of a daughter-in-law down by the Verde River. Wasn't that something worth crying about? I mean, if you give a damn about such things, isn't that all the reason in the world to fall to your knees and let everyone within earshot know you're good and upset? No sir, not a tear. None for Zoe and none for little Jackie. Not even as much as a whimper or a fart in my direction. She just turned her feet and shuffled back off into the darkness like I asked her. Smart bitch, for sure. I'd just finished replacing the two bullets missing from my Colt from splintering Zoe's kneecaps against the bedroom wall.

It didn't take long before I drifted off to sleep atop that porch. The cool, October breeze which carried the sweet desert scents of an approaching storm was like

STARVING ZOE

Mama's milk on parched lips. Yes sir, took me right off into dreamland without so much as a warning. Even Poon, still hitched to the post and blowing noisy gas like a rabid beast, wasn't enough to keep me on this plane of consciousness. It'd been a long day, after all. It's not a regular occurrence when a man leaves the terrors of war behind him, only to return home and brew a fresh pot of his own. Sure, I'd had my worries that Zoe had given up on me ever returning home and moved on, but I was hoping to high Hell that the whore had the decency to land inside someone else's house. Maybe even teepee! Isn't that what those Indians lived in? Teepees? Buffalo scrotum wrapped around some sticks or something like that? Either way, the bitch could've had the good will to pack up and move in with that fellow rather than lay her coot in our marriage bed. Not to mention letting that eerie Medicine Woman and infant stay there as well. No respect, I say. No respect whatsoever.

Anyway, while I was sitting out on the porch having dreams of dead wives and venom-stricken babies, it would seem that the Indian broad went and paid a visit to my sweet Zoe tied up to the Mesquite tree down by the Verde River. I thought for a fact my scorned bride was talking out of her arse when she claimed that Medicine Woman had powers and connections to the underworld and such. No sir, she wasn't making that part up at all. I should've known because, in the past, the bitch wasn't really all that creative. Sure, she'd made up her share of whoppers in her day, that Zoe Telos, but most of the time she was just playing off some of the things I'd said. Never was much to come up with imaginative rants all by herself. Now, this is the part of the story worth paying attention to, I guarantee. Never leave loose ends no matter how frayed the rope. Never.

At that moment, I could only imagine that their conversation on the banks of the Verde River went somewhere along the lines of this:

"Well hey there, Zoe Telos! What are you doing out here in the cold and tied up on the banks of the Verde River? You've got all kinds of thorns stuck off in you and it looks like it hurts to Hell and back."

"Well," old Zoe probably said back. "My husband came home from soldiering in the war and caught me being a cheating Indian fucker. Yes, he most certainly did! Took my no-good baby and threw the bitch down a well and then blew off both my kneecaps while I was laying in his bed. Even though I probably deserved all that and more, I'm kind of vexed about it. I truly am!"

"Damn, that's too bad," the Indian bitch more than likely continued. "Yeah, you may have been queen of the dirty prostitutes in the Northern Arizona Territory, but I don't think you deserved none of that. No ma'am, you sure didn't. I mean, he could've smacked you around a bit, but I don't think he needed to go and kill your baby and shoot off those creaky kneecaps. Would you like me to untie you?"

"No," Zoe probably replied. "I'm pretty much on the verge of death here and I already said my kneecaps was blown off so there's no way I could walk away too far from this here Verde River unless you wanted to carry me. By the look of you, I can tell you're just an Indian bitch and probably can't bear my cheating tail up the hill and through the desert. I know you Indians aren't that keen on scientific stuff like weight ratios and reattaching kneecaps, so I won't burden you with such things. I guess I'll just stay tied to this tree until a wolf or bear or something along those lines comes walking up and eats me. Dirty coot and all."

"Well, damn," the Indian would've said at that point. "It's a shame you feel that way, old Zoe Telos. I had really planned on putting those kneecaps back on you with a dirty handkerchief and a few drops of honey because that's the way our simple, red asses think sometimes. By any chance is there anything I could do for you to help you out in your current situation? Maybe some Indian magic to stir this situation up even further than it already is? Maybe conjure up some demonic powers for you?"

"Why sure," Zoe Telos would've answered. "That sounds mighty helpful of you, being an Indian Medicine Woman and all. Do you think you could send a spectral telegraph to Satan himself, bring forth the scourge of the underworld, and give my husband a real hard time? It sure would be much appreciated if you could do something like that."

Now, keep in mind that I'm only imagining how this conversation went and I'm sure I'm taking a ton of liberties when it comes to how intelligent of a talk this was. Just bear with me and we'll give them both the benefit of the doubt. You know how women folk get when the two of them start talking about crazy things. It goes all this way and that, then, the next thing you know, some evil stuff starts happening.

"You're in luck, Zoe," that mean bitch probably said. "I just happen to have a bunch of birds' eyes and monkey feet in a bag back at the teepee. I'm sure I could conjure up some previously unimaginable nonsense if I mixed them all together with some spit and blood. You'd probably look good as a Navajo Skin-walker, now that I mention it. How would you like that, Zoe? Do you want to be a Skin Walker to get revenge on that Robert Jack? Bird eyes, monkey feet, spit, and blood are all it takes. Maybe some piss, too!"

"Oh, I wouldn't want to put you out, Indian bitch," Zoe would claim. "No, I'd probably just better hang on this tree and die like the hooker I am. I wouldn't want to upset things or stir the pot. After all, Robert had been riding that cross-eyed horse for days through the desert just to get here. I wouldn't want to trouble him anymore than I already have. Thank you, though."

"Well, that's just too bad, Zoe Telos," the bitch would insist. "I've got all that stuff back in the teepee and I was going to do it, anyway. Yes ma'am, that's what I'm going to do whether you like it or not. I'm just going to mix up some bird's eyes, monkey feet, spit, piss, and blood and turn you into a Skin Walker. You just go pay a visit to Robert one last time and see how that fits you. Does that sound okay?"

Yes sir! I'm almost certain that's how it all went down at the banks of the Verde River. Poor wolves, bears, and whatever didn't even get a chance to snack on the flesh of that whore like I'd planned because the Indian woman cut her down to do everything she said she was going to do. You just can't change the mind of a woman once she gets to talking about revenge with monkey feet. Yep, probably gnawed through that old rope with her one good tooth and set my Zoe free to do her worst against a man who'd done not a whole lot wrong by modern standards. Probably took her back to the teepee and poured all kinds of ugly all over her and said some mumbo jumbo Indian words to seal the deal with the devil himself. Indian bitches are just creepy, they are. A whole separate kind of oddness when compared to the likes of white folks, I guarantee. Then again, white folks have a ton of problems. Hurts most of them like Hell to lift a finger for too damn long without having to call a Mexican or Black person to finish up. Lazy, entitled white folks was the reason I had to go away in the first place. Kind of hard for an Indian dick to sneak inside your favorite puss when it's currently occupied by your own cock, isn't it? Yes sir! Since I was in the middle of playing the blame game, I might as well go ahead and throw over privileged white people under the stagecoach too.

I knew something sinister was in the works because it got all kinds of quiet on the front porch of the homestead. The crickets stopped rubbing their legs together, and you could hear a pin drop from a dozen miles away in that desert. That's when you know something's coming for you in the middle of nowhere. It gets all quiet because the little critters can see it coming before you do. They're all in tune to nature, unlike people. I couldn't even hear the moths fucking anymore. Either they knew something was on its way or that one had blew his little moth load all over the lantern. Lucky little bug bastard. On top of that, they probably saw that bitch running top speed through the darkness as she was headed back home to make life difficult.

"There she goes," those crickets and moths probably said. "There goes Zoe Telos, headed home after having some Indian mumbo jumbo done to her. Yes sir, you can just see the blood, piss, and spit dripping off her as she's running on all fours like a freak of nature. Yep, that's a bird's eye and a monkey foot for sure!"

Now, keep in mind that I'm just kind of imagining how all this is going and taking a few liberties here and there with what's being stated. Really not that much different than when I was imagining the conversating between Zoe and that crusty Indian whore. Crickets are indeed interesting creatures, I've heard, and that's probably what they were all saying to one another. I'm sure all the lizards and snakes and shite put in their two cents, but surely none of them speak the same language. No, those crickets just brushed it off as a couple of lizards talking nonsense and kept on watching Zoe Telos run on all fours like some hairless animal with a birth defect. Absolutely, good sirs and ma'ams. It was as quiet outside as a church right before the preacher dunks the kid into the waters and you want to see if the devil spawn bursts into flames. Nothing at all was making any kind of sound. It was normally the kind of symphony which rich, city folk pay all kinds of money to see in places like New York or Boston. I never understood why they'd do something like that just to see someone in a suit blow on an inanimate object. Yes sir, used to watch that for free under the bridges in Brooklyn, and both the blower and blowee were alive. Anyway, it was quiet is what I'm trying to say. Quiet enough for me to sit up, take notice, and pull the Colt pistol from my belt in readiness. Something told me that my interactions with Zoe Telos and the Indian Medicine Woman weren't over just yet.

I peered out into the darkness but couldn't see much more than a bunch of blackness staring back at me. You see, the moon had been shrouded by some dense clouds from an approaching storm and I could barely see my hand in front of my face. The lights I'd lit in the living room weren't helping things too much either because they were shining through the windows. Basically, I didn't have the luxury of staring at whatever was staring back at me from the desert brush in the distance. No sir, I'd inadvertently created a beacon to whatever evil was prancing around out in the dark and there wasn't a whole hell of a lot I could do about it with only a moment's notice. Just then, a cauldron of bats rushed me from out of nothing, and I threw my hands to my face for protection. Goddamn blood suckers swarmed all around my head, tangling their tiny claws inside my hair and feasting, bite by bite, on the exposed flesh of my face. I could feel their tiny teeth tearing into me one by one like little, teasing hypodermic needles. I dropped the Colt to the ground out of desperation, not thinking anything of the greater evil who'd summoned the spawn from Hell in the first place. I swung like a mad man at the quick little devils, but it was no use. Trickles of my own blood poured from stinging facial wounds and I screamed into the darkness for assistance that'd never come to my aid.

No sir, the only thing who could hear my cries was someone who intended on making them more severe. More permanent. I ran for dear life into my home for protection only to realize all too late that I'd left my revolver on the front porch. That's when Zoe Telos showed her demonic face through the windowpane of the living room. I screamed again for good measure.

White as a ghost, she was. Sure, that's always been an overused figure of speech because most folks have never seen a real ghost or anything which truly resembles one. No sir, they just say it all the time without ever having anything to use as a true point of reference. To be honest, I don't believe I'd ever seen one either and am probably guilty of using that phrase a few too many times myself. Zoe Telos was as white as a ghost, for sure. When I'd left her tied to a tree on the banks of the Verde River, she still had all the color of a normal human being, at least one of the Caucasian persuasion, but the bitch staring at me with bared teeth and incensed demeanor was certainly as white as the mythical ghost most people discuss when utilizing that expression. The squeal of her skin against the glass was deafening as I backed desperately into the corner of my living room. To boot, I'd left my common sense somewhere in the vicinity of my porch along with my Colt revolver, because I failed to lock the door while escaping the bats. It didn't matter none. Zoe pressed her nightmare of a face deeper and harder into the windowpane as the cracks began to form. Dumb bitch wasn't even planning on using the unlocked door, anyway.

Inch by inch, her deformed head entered the window, causing slivers of glass to slice the once beautiful visage. Blood of an unnamed color poured atop the hardwood floor of the room as I quaked in trepidation, refusing to move from the corner I cowered in to await the inevitable. Suddenly, the glass all gave way simultaneously and her clawed hands reached indoors for better leverage. A lightning flash of blurred images brought her face to face with me once more. My darling bride who I'd left for dead on the banks of the old Verde River exhaled toxic fumes into my nasal cavities, and my stomach lurched forward. That was when the voice of pure evil came forth through the once poetic mouth of my undead girl.

"You can vomit and scream all you want, Robert Jack, but it's not going to help you any. You've unleashed the madness you now see before your eyes and it's not going away anytime soon. No, Robert Jack, this is all your doing, and I want to make sure you get your money's worth before it's all said and done."

"What in tarnation, Zoe!" My scream escaped. "What has that Indian bitch done to you?"

"What did the Indian do to me?" Zoe teased. "No, Robert Jack, this is all your doing. You've called forth the demon with your own actions and I'm here to deliver. I'm sure you've realized by now that every action upon this Earth has a consequence. I'm just here to show you the beginning of all things final in your life. After all, you weren't so kind to offer me the quickest of deaths, therefore I shall do the same for you. This, my husband, is only the beginning. Load your guns, sharpen your sticks, and run for the sake of your own existence. The end is coming for you. I'll be coming for you."

With that, Zoe turned her back to me, leaving all

things ugly she had on exhibit faced in the opposite direction. I scanned the room quickly for anything possible to be used as a weapon but my options were limited to nothing effective. In a show of desperation, I reached deep into the burning fireplace to pull a log to my defense. I could feel the needles of pain penetrating my exposed flesh, but it made no difference to me in the face of the monster now occupying my home. Bubbling flakes of my own skin pooled to the floor as I fought the instinct to drop it, leaving me defenseless once again. I ignored the impulse and held true to the plan. After a few drawn out seconds, I could no longer feel my hand. The acrid stench of burnt flesh filled the innards of my home. I knew it was my hand stinking because I hadn't cooked anything else since I'd been home. It was dead. A slave to the makeshift weapon I'd rescued from oblivion's flames. I entered a defensive stance and prayed for the best outcome.

"Come on, Zoe," I screamed in defiance. "Let's get this dance over with. I wasn't afraid of you in life, and I'm refusing to fear the ugly you've become!"

Zoe then cocked her head slightly to the side, only revealing half of the face she'd come to be. The smile she offered sent chills down my spine as I dropped the smoldering log to the floor. Fresh fuel from the living room rug brought the flames to life once again and spread to the closest curtains and upholstered furniture. Zoe laughed maniacally.

"I can see you haven't changed a bit and still have tons to learn, Robert Jack. I'm not here to kill you on this night. No, I'm just here to set the rules of the game yet to be played."

Starving Zoe

"Rules?" I asked, frantically. "What rules? Why don't you just get this all over with and face me now?"

"Because it's not your game, Robert Jack. It's mine. Enjoy what remains of your life during hours of sunlight, for I'll be returning when it sets once more. I'll return every night until my vengeance is satisfied. When I think you've had enough, I'll end it."

With that, my world faded to black. I awoke the next morning with the sunlight burning my scarred eyes fraction by fraction. As they adjusted, revealing no signs of the monstrous abomination from the night before, I began to wonder if the entire scenario had been some type of rage fueled nightmare brought on by the discovery of my unfaithful bride. Sure, I knew for a fact I'd killed the baby and tied Zoe to the tree. I also knew for sure I'd had a minimalist conversation with that Medicine Woman, too. What about the return of Zoe Telos, though? Had that been real as well? It wasn't until I began to settle my aching bones into a sitting position that I noticed my home was nothing more than a charred skeleton of memories. Luckily, the rainstorm I'd seen in the distance had made quick work of the housefire and left me alive to tell the tale. That was also about the time I noticed the dead, split flesh of my blackened left hand as well. Unusual in such a situation, I felt no pain impulses screaming to my brain for healing. Actually, I felt nothing at all. Yes sir, it was truly gone and nothing more than a deadened decoration to adorning the remainder of my working body parts. Luckily, I pretty much did everything, including shoot the Colt revolver, with my right hand. It was sure to make reloading, riding, and everything else a man must do in this crazy world a little more difficult than normal, but at least I could still live and fight back if necessary. My awakening in the world of frightening tomorrows wasn't all bad. Then, I laid eyes on Poon.

The horse didn't have so much as a fighting chance when it came time for his initial face to face with Zoe Telos. As of this moment, his cross-eyed head lay unattached from his shoulders atop the rain-soaked ground of the desert. I was having difficulty determining if she'd used those clawed hands of hers to do it or if she'd gnawed the thing off by biting, but the poor fellow now sat atop a pool of his own blood which collected in an impact crater of mud and such caused by the fall. A line of ants, beetles, and other tiny creatures of the desert floor battled amongst themselves as they fed upon the horse's internal organs. The realization soon hit me that I was now horseless, bootless, and homeless in the unforgiving Arizona Territory. My hat was in the house, too! It's hard to be a cowboy without a hat. For sure, just ask any desert dweller you come upon in this day and age and they'll be glad to tell you that you've got to have a hat! At least my gun had managed to remain unharmed in last night's chaos. I tucked it into the welcoming holster with a rehearsed, frictionless slide realizing the only ammunition not burned to the point of uselessness in last night's fire was what I had tucked into the individual loops of my gun belt. Maybe a bit in Poon's saddle bag, too. Easily just forty rounds to fend off the creature promised to return upon the setting of the sun. Just like them soldiers at the Battle of Vicksburg. From what I recalled, that didn't work out too well for those poor sons of bitches.

Starving Zoe

Yes sir, I was surely going to die. It was no longer a matter of 'if' but 'when.' How long could I defend myself from this scorned creature of the night barefooted, exposed, and with only a couple handfuls of bullets?

As I dug through the pockets of my saddlebags still attached to Poon's headless corpse, I began to inspect the porch for any signs of the previous night's bat invasion. Not a single drop of bat droppings or evidence littered the porch of my former home lending validity to the notion that the encounter was all in my head. Was that even possible? I could feel the rising sun's heat tickle the blood-stained scars on my face as though they were an actual existence, but I had no mirror at my disposal to back it up. How in the name of all that was real and obtainable in this crazy, mixed up world was Zoe able to make me believe I was being attacked by bats on my own front porch? Sure enough, I should've put a bullet into the red forehead of that Indian bitch before she made her way to the banks of the Verde River. No sir, idiot Robert Jack had to sit there on the porch and taunt her with obscenities and nonsense rather than finish the job the way the Army had taught him to do on countless occasions. I shook that thought out of my head as quickly as it came, I most certainly did! I was the failed end of many things in this world, but I sure wasn't a bad soldier. A bad husband, a murderer, and a convenient liar from time to time? Certainly. A bad soldier? Never. The intelligent training of the best superiors the Confederate Army had to offer made sure of that. I was sworn to swallow my anxiety and fight this bitch to the bitter end for certain.

C. Derick Miller

I cautiously crept down to the banks of the Verde River carrying every single possession I had available to me in this world. As expected, the ropes I'd tied around Zoe's bleeding, naked body hung without a prize within the tangled branches of the Mesquite tree. Near the base of that tree was indeed the unidentifiable footprints of a being I hoped never to see again but knew for sure would be hunting my worthless soul upon sundown. I dipped the remnants of my left hand into the frigid, flowing waters only to realize it was a useless gesture. Other than the flaking of a few chunks of dead skin now washing away into God knows where, nothing caused any sense of life to return to the useless limb. Not even so much as a tickle or twinge of pain came from the inoperative appendage now dangling from my left wrist. The insanity in me almost wished to cut it free from its mooring and send it down the swift waters of the Verde like a dislodged, useless branch ripped asunder from the mighty tree to which it once belonged. A logical, pain-fearing remainder told me to leave it alone. Hell, I'd probably pass out from the sight of my own spurting blood, leaving myself an easy target for Zoe's inevitable return. No sir. If it was a fight she was wanting, it was a fight she was sure to get.

I sat there on the banks of the river and filled my mouth full of bullets like the warrior I truly was. One by one, I spit them into the empty slots of my revolver using my tongue as a guiding tool. Clicking it shut, I shoved it deep into its awaiting holster once more and hopped to my bare feet to begin the trek in the direction of potential food, shelter, and assistance. North was my best bet, for certain. San Francisco peak was now in view from the rising sunlight and all signs pointed to its jagged protrusions as the only sure way to have a fighting chance against the supernatural harbinger of doom certain to pick up on my trail. Hell hath no fury like a woman scorned, or so I've been told. In hindsight, curses to whoever said that for the first time and had the circles at their disposal to spread such nonsense. For sure, they'd never seen the pale face of their dead wife peeking in through the cracked window of their once loving home with a brain full of vengeful agenda.

CHAPTER FOUR

WEDNESDAY
IN THE PINES

A SKIN WALKER. Yes sir, that's what all the local legends called them. I remember hearing the Navajo Indians speak of them in whispers when Zoe and I first made it down to the Arizona Territory. Since we were outsiders to their culture, the Navajo never clued us in on their origin or their abilities . . . but it would appear as though a certain Medicine Woman broke that taboo. A pale skinned, bean pole, long necked, clawed hand, greasy haired, half naked anomaly conjured up with blood, spit, and piss. Hell, the Indian whore didn't even bother throwing in clothes on her either. No sir! Just the sheet from our bed half tied around Zoe's waist like one of them old Greek fellows in the New York bath houses. I'm not even going to speak about her breasts. Skinny little things appeared as though someone was smuggling eggs in a worn-out sock. Definitely not the tits I left behind. A damn shame, it was. A damn shame!

It's strange, really. Most of the Indians were

scared to death of the repercussions which came along with betraying their own secrets, but that witch just went ahead and twisted the rules into something evil. Much like the werewolves the Brits and French back on the East Coast would describe once they got a few pints down in them, the skin walkers were part man and part animal. Many nights, I would sit and listen to them whimper about the loss of a loved one or how they barely escaped from the clutches of a werewolf on the moors beneath a full moon. Sure, most people in attendance just played it off as lunacy brought on by the drink, but I knew better. I could see true terror in their eyes as they recapped the horrifying moments. Irish werewolves were the exact opposite from their folklore. They were more like protectors rather than murderers, but I can't say I'd ever met one personally. Navajo skin walkers? Totally different. Pure, vengeful evil.

With what I could gather from multiple, half-assed, cryptic conversations among the true locals, a skin walker was summoned or created to pursue revenge on someone who'd done wrong. Once that evil spirit settled in, the person you knew was completely gone. No sir, not like a werewolf at all. No back and forth or waking up in a field with your dick hanging out for the whole world to see. Just straight up, unadulterated evil from sundown to sunrise. That's exactly why I'd spent the majority of my first day on the run hiding like a beaten puppy from a strap in this cave I'd found in the pine forest. If I was going to have to fight that bitch all night long, I would need some good sleep, for sure. After all, it's not like I still had a house and a comfortable bed to snuggle in. No sir. Mean bitch took away my pussy, ruined my bed, and burned both stories of my house to the ground. Even burned a worn-out guitar I'd won in a poker game from some poor logger right before I was pushed off into the Army. I was just learning to pick at it decent when the judge came knocking. In hindsight, I'm pretty pissed off about losing that damn guitar. I had every intention of learning to pick that thing on the front porch. Also, now that I'm thinking back a spell, I was the idiot who pulled the flaming log out of the fireplace. I've got this black, useless hand to prove it. Damn it all! That was my fingering hand. Never mind. Just send it all to Hell. Anyway, that bitch was coming, and I needed rest.

So, back to the inevitable matter at hand—my only good one Zoe must've somehow convinced that Indian bitch to turn her into this skin walker thingamajig and now she was out for revenge. Ultimately, it should be me walking around looking like a freak of nature because I'm not the one who did anything wrong. Zoe Telos was the one letting every red man in the territory come by and take a tag at her coot, right? All I did was come home from the war with the Yankees. Absolutely, all I did was ride that poor cross-eyed horse through the desert for weeks in hopes of finding some fraction of my former life waiting with open arms and spread legs. Is that too much to ask for a beat down son of a bitch like myself? I truly think not. Yes sir, I know for a fact that some meaner men have returned to their beds and received a lot more than that. My favorite pussy, bed, house, guitar, and left hand were now distant remnants of my past with no way to get any of them back. Hell, I was even mad about Poon, the cross-eyed, equine head case. Sure, he was as dumb as a box full of used leper dicks, but at least he listened to me when I felt like talking. Never tried to kill me, either. Got his cock caught between a couple of rocks once, but never tried to kill me. Then, I remembered my boots.

Barefoot in the Arizona Territory wasn't a good thing to be, especially during the month of October. At some point, the snow was going to hit San Francisco peak and start trickling its way down into the valley. I would freeze to death for sure, making my feet look something along the lines of this bunk left hand. They'd rot off from frostbite after too long and then I'd be on my belly, trying to get away from Zoe Telos like a snake on the desert floor. Spending an hour or so complaining about my current situation didn't cause me to like my chances of survival too much. If the elements contained in my final, ignorant choice for a homestead didn't kill me off, my scorned wife truly would. I wasn't even sure if an apology would do much good the next time she and I ran across each other. Then again, you'd have to possess a heart for that apology to mean something, and that black thing of hers was probably gone as well. Nasty Indian bitch probably had to eat it to make Zoe the white-faced freak who entered my living room last night. Goddamn Indian witch and her friendship to the denizens of the underworld probably made damn sure to drain the life, blood, and soul out of my bride before sending her my direction. I sure didn't feel any love going on in those eyes when she cornered me.

My mind was too frantic to continue sleeping so I began packing what few belongings I had left into

Poon's saddle bag. It was my saddle bag now, I guessed. Yes sir, just strap that uncomfortable thing to my back and carry on into the wilderness like a beast of burden. At least my eyes weren't crossed, and I never found rocks attractive. I'd managed to salvage most of the rope I had used to tie Zoe to the Mesquite tree down by the Verde River. Either that Indian whore had gnawed through it with her one good tooth or Zoe used those rancid fingernails to get out of it. Still, I had a pretty good amount coiled up in Poon's saddle bag and was sure I'd be needing it at some point. If there's anything that the city of Boston taught me, it was that you could always use a good bit of rope in a tight spot. It was like the city's motto or something along those lines. Sons of bitches always talking about it like rope was the greatest damned invention since the outhouse! Next to that was a trusty pocketknife I'd had since my teenage years. Yes sir, I'd carried that sharp little sticker with me from New York, to Arizona, and to war and back. Never had I let it out of my sight, and I wasn't about to start tonight. It was sharp as all Hell, but the blade was just long enough to make Zoe Telos get a good laugh if I tried to stick her with it. Absolutely not. No compensation going on with that pocketknife whatsoever. Then there was a beat-up box containing a few bullets for the Colt pistol. Six in the cylinder, twelve on my belt, and twenty-two from the saddle bag. Forty rounds, just like I thought. The Battle of Vicksburg all over again. Finally, there was an apple. Just one apple.

Yes sir, that's all there was left as far as food went in my personal belongings and it wasn't looking none too good. If I didn't eat it tonight, then I was certain the delicious morsel wouldn't make it to the sunrise. Then again, I was still certain I wouldn't make it until sunrise either, so I started to eat the thing out of spite. Old Zoe chased me out of my house so quick that I didn't get a chance to pack any jerky or whatever else my bitch wife and the Indian crew had lingering in the kitchen. Unfortunately, the Arizona Territory wasn't too keen on fruit bearing trees, so hunger would be a definite issue within the very near future. Sure, I could stand in the middle of the Verde River with my tiny pocketknife until the dumbest fish in the history of fish randomly swam into the blade, but time was becoming an issue. A snake would bite me before I could even get the blade anywhere near something vital and a bear or wolf would laugh themselves to death. Perhaps that was the answer. Pull out my puny knife in the face of a predator and hope they killed themselves from the humorous sight. Hell yes, Mr. Wolf, I'm standing here with this tiny knife but I'm the one still standing and breathing. Laugh away, Mr. Wolf. Laugh away. Yes sir, I was either going to starve, freeze to death with bare feet, or get ripped to pieces by the skin walker named Zoe Telos. Fortunate me, I guess. All this luck with no poker games in sight. The story of Robert Jack's life.

The sun began to disappear below the hilly horizon of my portion of the Arizona Territory, so I sucked the lone apple down to the core like it was paying me to do so. One less thing to carry in the grand scheme of things. Sure, it wasn't like that piece of nearly rotted fruit was taking up too much space in the saddle bag, I just didn't need to accidentally grab it instead of the bullet box when death started flying. I couldn't help but imagine if that, too, wouldn't be the mother of all bitches. Ducking behind a rock or tree for a quick reload in the heat of battle against the supernatural, cheating forces of Zoe Telos and shoving an apple into my gun instead of a bullet? For sure, that reminded me of some devilish misfortune that would happen when things began to get a little hairy. Absolutely. I was certainly glad that half rotted apple was no longer a thorn in my side dwelling in Poon's saddle bag. A miniscule smile began to creep across my tired face with the thoughts of sticking that apple in my gun, but it was soon erased by a falling raindrop. Precise as an Army surgeon, that single raindrop smacked me right in the middle of my smiling lips and journeyed down the right side of my mouth. Then came another. Then another. Soon, it was a precipitated free for all on the face of the Jacker. This is when that hat would've come in handy for sure. Yes sir, add the search for shelter onto the survival list along with food, boots, weapons, a hat, a horse, and an apology letter to the underworld for even coming home to this God forsaken nightmare.

Then, I heard it. Old Zoe Telos wasn't wasting any time, that was for damn sure! The last of the fading sunlight had just snuck below the horizon and the first star of the night sky peered down at me through the rain clouds out of curiosity. A screech the likes of which I'd only heard once before in my life echoed throughout the pines with only a single member of humanity in attendance for its nocturnal, debut concert. The time had come to defend myself or die trying. After all, I had to make sure I gave that lone star in the sky a show it wouldn't soon forget. Lucky star. I had to admit, it was a pretty good seat to have when oblivion's traveling circus came to town. I would've traded seats without question.

The pitter patter of rain on the dried needles of the pine forest made me eerily aware that all Hell was about to break loose in my general vicinity. I glared into the darkness for any available signs of Zoe but got nothing but blackness and shadows in return. Sneaky little bitch was probably breathing over my shoulder as I was thinking this, but I didn't want to turn my head to find out. Then, a slight stir in the underbrush asked me to look down at my bare feet for reassurance. What I witnessed almost made me wish for the bats I'd had to deal with on the night before back on the porch of my burned-up house.

Even though the shadows of the night blended in well with the darkened color scheme, it was easily a six-footer. Knowing what I'd learned about rattlesnakes since choosing to reside in the Southwest corner of this country, its length meant it already had me dead to rights if it chose to strike me on my exposed feet. Yes sir, the damn thing was already nuzzling the big toe of my left foot as though it wanted to take it somewhere private and do a bit of good snake fucking. Now, I'd never seen a snake fuck before, but I knew good and well it happened from time to time, otherwise there wouldn't be any little snakes squirming around in the woods. I'd never seen it with my own eyes, but I'd often wondered how they did it. The theory of a snake dick escaped me altogether. Wouldn't they get chaffed from rubbing it around on everything when they crawled? Maybe that was why the critters were so mean-tempered to begin with! Snake vagina? That was easy to comprehend. With my most recent of discoveries, all vaginas had snakes attached to them. We just choose to call them women.

So, as this slithering nightmare continued to snuggle with the big toe on my left foot like it intended on getting married, I used my one good hand to pull the Colt revolver from its belt and clicked back the hammer as quietly as possible. Quiet obviously meant nothing to this creature because it picked up on what I was trying to do almost instantly. Coiling back on itself, the snake began to shake its tail with a tell-tale warning. The English language is a work of art, isn't it? The buzzing was almost deafening but I didn't dare cover my ears out of fear of what it might do to my feet, legs, and crotch if left unprotected. Unprotected? What in the hell was I even thinking? I was sure to be dead as a doornail if the thing chose to bite me anywhere at all. Did I believe for a second that stopping this thing with one of my hands could be considered a safer alternative? No sir, my Colt was the only solution to the puzzle in which I was currently entangled so I pushed the barrel more toward the rattler for better accuracy. If I happened to miss the arshole with the first shot, there'd be little reason for firing off a second. We stared one another down to see who had big enough balls to make the first move. Snake balls. Yet another mystery in my personal world of odd thoughts at inappropriate times.

I kept noticing that the rattler was less concerned about me as a person and suddenly more interested in the gun I held tightly in my right hand. What in the blazes did a rattlesnake know about the weaponry of men? Was the creepy, crawly little serpent aware of what it was so infatuated with? That was when my brain's warning bell sounded and I realized this was no ordinary snake who'd been nuzzling the big toe on my left foot. I attempted to jump backward to distance myself from the annoying extension to Satan's cock just as the initial strike came. I say initial because I knew this thing was going to have a go at me repeatedly until it was satisfied. Just like the night before, this creature was in total control of the remainder of my life because it, indeed, was no ordinary snake. I could see a glint of a spectral, personal touch in its eyes as it stared at me curiously. Zoe Telos had managed to turn herself into a snake and a bat so far during our brief dance of fate. There was obviously a lot more to this whole skin walker thing than previously imagined by my feeble mind. Tripping backward over a fallen branch, I landed hard upon my back on the forest floor leaving myself open for the creature's next attack. I thrust my hand forward out of instinct to give myself any type of protection imaginable, no matter how insane, and closed my eyes tight for the worst. I felt the unimaginably hard hit of the snake against my flesh but no pain. Slowly, I opened one eye to the carnage I knew for sure was taking place between the animal and my own body . . . and laughed.

"Zoe Telos, you're not going to get too much pleasure out of that burned up hand! That meat is dead to the world and I'm not feeling anything whatsoever! Just gnaw away on it like there's no tomorrow because there ain't nothing happening on my end. Go on and get you a mouth full of that crusty thing!"

The snake paused its activity and glared up at me with obvious hatred. Slowly, almost in a display of embarrassment, the creature released its bite, tucking the retractable fangs back into its disgusting mouth. It coiled up once more at my feet and began to rattle its tail with fierce velocity. It was now or never.

"Goddamn, Zoe!" I chuckled. "That must've tasted something along the lines of a piece of chicken that slipped off the spit and into the fire. You'll definitely want something to drink after that to get the taste out of your mouth, for sure. Would the lead from this gun suffice? Drink up, bitch!"

I placed one right between the eyes of that rattlesnake as the Colt revolver filled the surrounding air with its deafening pop and a nose stinging scent of something only to be described as heaven to a soldier. She coiled and flopped on the forest floor as though I'd really done a bit of damage to the girl . . . but I knew better. I reckoned it was all for show in hopes I'd turn my back for an uneducated flight further into the woods. No such luck, Zoe Telos. No ma'am, I wasn't about to give you the benefit of striking me dead in the arse. Not on this night! I aimed the pistol for a second volley just as the snake stopped its seizure. The animal recoiled back into a defensive position and locked eyes with me once more. This time, the most awful voice escaped its mouth, causing me to stumble backward through the brush and fallen foliage even more than before. Nothing could've prepared me for the human voice gliding across the lips of a snake. Nothing at all.

STARVING ZOE

Raindrops in my ears were drowning out everything except the evil.

"Oh, Robert Jack, you think you know it all, don't you?" the gurgling words came. "Yes, there's a lot more to what I've become than I'll ever allow you to know during this dwindling life of yours. As I'm sure you've discovered, those bullets can't stop me. You're at the mercy of the ancients now, Mr. Jack. You're at my mercy!"

The speaking snake reared up on its tail and stood straight and stiff as a board. It began to glow with a blinding luminance only to be described as not of this world. I placed my blackened left hand atop my forehead to shield my vision from the intensifying radiance but never removed the aim of my weapon from the foul creature at my feet. With a flash, the naked, pale image of Zoe Telos stood before me in all her deceased glory once more. She gritted her teeth as though the mother of all headaches had made camp inside her skull and forced a sinister growl in my direction. With a moist, disturbingly audible stir, the bullet I'd fired into the head of the snake wriggled from its home in her ghostly face and landed at my feet with a thump. No sir, this bitch Zoe Telos wasn't lying one bit when it came to how helpless I truly was from now until the end of my days upon this Earth. Her unusually lengthy limbs slapped me to the ground where she straddled and trapped me on all sides. I was now her unwilling prisoner between those gangly legs. The pines appeared to stare down upon me in shivering anticipation.

"Oh, Robert, it's just like I told you last night," she whispered softly into my ear as though we were still friends enjoying a romp in the sack. "Weren't you paying attention? Did you not believe me? I told you that you wouldn't get out of this situation alive and I meant it all the way. You killed my child and then left me for dead on the banks of the Verde River. Did you think you'd get away with this atrocity without suffering the repercussions? This is just day number two, sweetheart. You and I have many dances left between us and the band responsible for the tunes is just getting warmed up. What shall we do first?"

My mind raced with a million possible answers but none that wouldn't get me killed, or at least extremely injured, among the rain and darkness of the Arizona pine forest. I could see the reflection of my terrified face in the opaque ocular pools she once called eyes. They were both like mirrors into my soul's hourglass, revealing the approaching end with every passing moment. The milk white skin surrounding Zoe's unusual skeletal structure seemed thin, almost transparent in certain parts. Her elongated appendages reminded me more of an animal who'd venture on all fours rather than the tradition human form I once spooned on cold nights between warm blankets. I was both disgusted and amazed simultaneously. My mouth refused to utter sympathy or awe toward the heinously deformed freak who straddled me helpless on the ground.

"Honestly, Zoe," I began without hesitation. "I couldn't imagine doing another thing with you and it has little to do with the fact that you're all dead and freaky looking out here in the woods. It has little to do with you turning into a snake and biting my blackened hand or sending your army of bats to feast on my face while I cowered in dread on the porch of our home. It has everything to do with you fucking that Indian bastard and letting him knock you up in the confines of our bedroom. I'm a man with morals, you dingy bitch, and I don't think I'll be getting over that anytime soon. So, just go ahead and get tonight's encounter over with. Do whatever it is you're going to do until the sun comes up so I can get good and ready for the trickery you're going to pull on me tomorrow night!"

It was at that exact moment when I realized Zoe Telos was far from amused with my accusations and banter. She shoved her face further into mine, revealing sharpened, pointed teeth only inches from my tear-blurred eyes. I'm sure she could sense the horror building within me in the same way as her rancid breath emblazing my soul through two unfortunate nostrils. She then sat high atop my chest, using her clawed hands as leverage on my shoulders. A look of utter seriousness spread across her pale face while she glared down at me, emotionless. Whatever she had planned was about to commence and I braced myself for the worst.

"As you wish, Robert Jack," she stated with minimal expression. "As you wish."

The air was forced from my lungs as she pinned my chest to the ground with the strength of ten men. She'd managed to unhinge the buttons of my pants with the other and searched frantically for my dick like a kid reaching for the last piece of hard candy at the bottom of the General Store barrel. I had no idea if her intentions were to rip the thing off or squeeze it until the head popped, but I wasn't allowing her any assistance with the activity. No sir, my cock had long since shriveled up into nothing the minute I'd seen her ghostly, naked body appear before my eyes. If her arms and legs were extremely longer than what was humanly acceptable, then you can imagine what that type of supernatural elongation had done to her tits. There was nothing remotely attractive regarding her naked form anymore and my stick was quite aware of it from the get-go. Unsuccessful in her endeavors, she decided to take more drastic measures.

The skin walker I once knew as my wife held me aloft, then slammed me hard into the rigid bark of the closest pine. Flakes of the majestic tree's protection burst through my shirt and into the flesh of my back as she scrubbed the skin from my body. Bleeding from the newly formed, gaping wounds, I winced as she removed my pants with a single swipe of her free hand. With a sensation that can only be compared to rumbling of the overhead thunder on that stormy night, she slammed me to the ground once more. As though some previously unknown force had taken control of my dick, it sprang to life in her chilled hand. A toothy smile spread on Zoe's face and she hungrily placed it between her lips. With each bob of her deceased head, the shaft of my penis penetrated her otherworldly throat and I fought any expression of pleasure my body intended on releasing out of pure habit. Her throat felt frozen as she forced me to explore it deeper. Total opposite of the sensation I'd expect to experience when placed in such a formerly arousing situation. Confused the hell out of my poor dick! That was when she obviously became bored with her oral fixation and performed the most unspeakable act imaginable.

STARVING ZOE

The flesh of my cock battled the confines of its own casing and grew painfully to a previously unobtainable length and size. Satisfied, Zoe forced my engorged phallus into her puss and howled loudly into the echoing darkness. The lips of her gash ground the flesh around my pubic area like the bark of the tree which'd torn my back up prior to this heinous act of courting. I painfully screamed in hopes she'd lighten up, but it only caused her to dig into me harder. I could feel the muscles of her vagina tightening with every rise and fall of her putrid pelvis as it tore my skin with every twitch. She held her head high into the pouring rain, never removing her hand from my crying face, and fucked me harder, faster, ignoring my plea for relief. I could sense the decomposing slime of her insides seep into my surrounded, torn cock, bringing to life a painful sensation resembling the rumored fires of Hell all around my pelvic area.

"Don't you like this, Robert Jack?" Zoe moaned with otherworldly pleasure. "Didn't you miss this pussy while you were fighting off all those Yanks? Don't you still love me?"

"Just fuck me and get it over with!" I plead through clenched teeth.

With that, she bore down harder onto my throbbing penis and cackled maniacally like a witch on a sex spree. I felt the spastic muscles of her cunt choke the circulation from my tattered dick as her vaginal lubricant increased, signaling her ongoing orgasm. At that point, I could no longer help it as well. My dick came to life, spraying the insides of my deceased bride with semen. My hands dug deep into the rocky mud of the saturated Arizona forest as I felt the most unusual sense of pleasure induced disgust imaginable to the human psyche. Zoe sat atop me, motionless as the wetness brought on by our cursed activity ventured down every slash, crack, and crevice of my lower extremities.

"Thank you, Robert Jack," she began, almost exhibiting sincerity. "You have no idea how much that meant to me."

Speechless from the supernatural raping of my body which had just taken place, I faded in and out of consciousness. The flames of her vaginal activity quieted atop my degloved penis as the remainder of my body fell uselessly and helplessly limp. For certain, I felt the remainder of my fractured skin tear away as she stood, still dripping a mixture of sperm and blood atop my still pulsing thighs. The surrounding air stung my exposed, raw flesh as my brain attempted to wrap around the idea of what had just taken place on the forest floor. With yet another blinding flash, the image of a satisfied Zoe Telos disappeared from sight, only to leave me writhing in pain and confusion alone. I'd completely forgotten about the Colt revolver held tightly in my trembling hands. As far as I was concerned, the death she teased couldn't arrive soon enough. The horrible creature had raped me of my seed and vanished as though I was some two-dollar whore handing out pokes on a half-priced Tuesday. The blackness of my subconsciousness took over as the early morning embers of sunlight shot daggers at me through the dense trees of the forest. Uncontrollable sleep soon arrived, bringing sexual nightmares with undead partners into my tainted mind. If I did manage to live through any inevitable future encounters with Zoe Telos, I feared the outcome. I let go of the gun before any irrational thoughts of ultimate finality surfaced in my unconsciousness.

CHAPTER FIVE
THURSDAY
THIRST COMES FIRST

I **AWOKE SOMEWHERE** near the noon hour because the sun was shining directly into my tired eyes. The Autumn breeze through the trees of the pine forest teased my exposed genitals but I refused to peek at the horror below my belt. Honestly, I knew without looking. I was alive, so far, but my left hand and dick had sure seen better days. Zoe was taking me apart piece by piece.

Wrapping what remained of my peeled penis into a torn remnant of my military issued shirt, I slowly pulled my trousers to my waist and secured them with their bloodstained brass buttons. I could feel it pulse with every heartbeat, revealing that life still resided in my dick . . . but you'd be surprised what you could live through. What in the hell was life, anyway? Honestly, I'd spent much of mine dealing death to others and this was my obvious repayment. War-torn nightmares, cheating wives, illegitimate children, a useless hand, a slaughtered cock, and an evil bitch on the verge of completing her agenda outweighed the miniscule dirty deeds of my youth. Yes sir, by a long shot, I thought. Still, karma was indeed a scorned whore and I was paying for every dance with body parts rather than coins. It wouldn't be much longer before life escaped me if my dues continued to increase.

Slowly, I made my way out of the dense trees and back to the open banks of the Verde River. My thirst had begun to overpower me shortly after my hike began and it was the only logical solution. Sure, I had to consider that what I was drinking was an unhealthy concoction of piss and whatnot from the animals and loggers who resided on the mountain, but my throat couldn't care less. I leaned carefully to the edge of the rushing water and sucked its life-giving essence for refreshment. My insides sang the hymns of dim-witted angels given the state of things inside my body, but they were hymns, nonetheless. I didn't even care if the tune was all wrong. Sing, you inbreds. Sing!

New life began to flow through to my beaten limbs with each gulp of the frigid, crystal clear water. Suddenly, a shadow pierced my peripheral view between the aquatic sparkle and sunlight's glisten. I reached for my pistol without so much as a pause in my drink. This time, I'd remember to shoot whatever was unlucky enough to interrupt my daytime privacy.

"She must really have it in for you, Robert Jack," spoke the Indian Medicine Woman who'd recently been forcefully evicted from my home. "I thought for sure she would've killed you by now."

"No, you old bitch," I responded with a growl. "It would appear as though Zoe enjoys her little games of cat and mouse much more than finality. She fucked the dick right off me, she did! Is that skin walker etiquette, or some God-awful disease that red, home-wrecking son of yours dished out when he impregnated her with that snake food at the bottom of my well? How in the name of all that is native and stinky do you speak English so well? I thought all you people did was grunt and point."

The Indian chuckled. Probably more at my misfortune rather than my crafty ability to crack wise, but it was still laughter. Hard to believe she still possessed any sense of humor after losing her squat house, daughter in law, and grandchild in one single evening. Seemed only fair that I put an end to her misfortunes in the very near future. After all, I had all those polished, shiny bullets and nothing much to kill on this annoyingly bright October day. I ultimately decided to just let the whore ramble in hopes she'd clue me in on some secret skin walker solutions. I motioned with my blackened hand for her to hurry forward with her latest bout of bitching.

"Mr. Jack, I've been living among white people for so long I've almost forgotten my native tongue. It all seems to come back to me from time to time when I run into one of my own, but those instances are few and far between. No, your kind has all but exterminated my race, but I've learned to adapt to the changes. Overcome the hardships. I was living a pretty comfortable, protected life in a nice home with a family until you came riding up on that cross-eyed horse."

"Poon!" I screamed angrily. "His name was Poon. Don't you dare speak ill against that creature because he bore me halfway across this God-forsaken country on his back while undergoing some unusual difficulties. Drinking his own piss and getting his cock caught between rocks and all. Me sitting atop his back the entire time must've made those activities even more problematic, if not somewhat less enjoyable. He deserved more thanks than having his own head torn away by my spastic, half dead wife."

The Medicine Woman glared at me impatiently as though she was waiting for a lull in my rant to continue the whining. Taking one last sip of water and a deep breath, I rolled over onto my back to stare the wench down. A better view of her would make it much easier when the time arrived to put a bullet into her dirt covered, emotionless face. Still, I refused to use my Colt yet. I wanted to hear more of what this magical mistress had to say. Eventually, she'd get irritated with my banter and reveal Zoe's potential weakness. At least I hoped she would. I'd hate to know I was carrying on a useless conversation with the wind bag instead of giving her a well-deserved whistle hole in her forehead.

"Are you finished, Mr. Jack?" the bitch inquired. "The sun sinks lower with every passing second and your time to run draws near. Why do you even bother fighting back? You know you can't win against the forces of darkness. You're just delaying the inevitable and, if I were you, I'd just sit right here by this river and let Zoe Telos have her way with you one last time. Don't fight back, don't resist, and don't scream for help. No one would come to your aid even if they heard you."

The Indian was right. Damn my decision to build so far away from civilization. I mean, I like my privacy and all, but I never once thought I'd have a freak of dark nature attempt to play me a tune on my skin flute. A little musical procession on the meat whistle, if you will. I was attempting to add humor into the situation which played over and over again horrifically in my mind, but it wasn't helping things all that much. Every pulse of the blood through my veins caused my dick to throb in pain and I dared not look at it again. Ever. If I had to take a piss, I would just do it in my pants. Catching a glimpse of that thing spraying around in all directions like stray rain clouds in a summer monsoon was more than enough to make me wish she'd just screwed it all the way into a nub. At least that would be somewhat comical to look at; maybe even circus worthy. I could still make a little money here and there in the traveling shows as the man who'd lost his cock to the devil. I'd pay to see it, wouldn't you? Don't lie. Of course you would. If not, I'd front someone the cash to see it and they could've paid me back at a later date. I said I'd go see it. I never said I'd go see it alone. That'd be some scary looking fuel for nightmares later in life!

"I don't need anyone's help, you crazy witch," I assured her. "When she gets here tonight, I plan on filling that whore so full of lead that I'd be able to use her tits as writing instruments! Yes ma'am, pluck her up off the cold ground and create a novel for the hell of it. Start something out along the lines of 'once upon a time there was this man with a cock which resembled a happy sunflower on a chilly morning . . . '. You know, poetic words like that. Then, I'm going to break her up into little tiny pieces and bury her all over the Arizona territory in a dozen or so shallow graves. I'd like to see that tricky bitch come back after doing something like that, I certainly would!"

The Indian lady doubled over in laughter at my expense. At least, I was almost sure it was at my expense. Normally, no one laughs at me face to face. Sure, they probably just waited until I was long gone and then gave it a good go, but never did they do so while I was still in their presence. It was kind of a dead giveaway that the lady was indeed having a good chuckle in my direction because I was the only person anywhere near where the two of us were having our back and forth. Pretty straight forward and simple mathematics if you ask me. Not bad for a son of a bitch who didn't attend school, right? Absolutely, if I do say so myself. The only thing I was ever truly educated in was the arts. The art of killing, to be more specific. It was about time I got on with my lessons. The conversation was getting overly long and ultimately tired. Still, I hung on for dear life in hopes of getting that one hint to save what remained of my life. My dick was beyond help. Probably would have to tie some ribbon around it to keep it from flapping in the breeze. I'm getting off track, though. She was looking at me like I was dancing along the borders of insanity. I let her continue, but with caution.

"Mr. Jack, how do you expect to kill something which doesn't die?"

"Kill?" I responded. "Lady, I already know damned well that I have no hope of truly killing this bitch that you've imbued with so much power. I've felt what she's capable of and, if you don't believe me, I can jerk down these trousers of mine and give you a glimpse into the true eye of horror. I honestly don't want to look at it but, if you truly insist, I'd give you a peek. She fucked the skin right off me and didn't so much as flinch. Held me in place like I was a helpless child on the verge of a temper tantrum and being restrained by an irritated, tired parent. All I'm really trying to say is that I know Zoe Telos will never truly die. You got the 'something' part right, though. She is no longer a 'someone'. She's a something. It's about time I began treating her like a 'something' and not the 'someone' I once loved."

The Indian tilted her head to the side as though I'd stuck a nerve deep down within her soul or surprisingly made a miniscule amount of sense. She blinked slowly in my direction and parted her lips one last time.

"Fair enough, Mr. Jack. Fair enough."

With that, she ascended the bank of the Verde River and disappeared from my sight. I drank deeply of the cool waters one more time as the last speck of sunlight faded behind the horizon. A familiar screech echoed through the pine forests up the mountain, and I knew that the next chapter in the game for my life was due to begin. What kind of voodoo magic was interfering with the sun? The hours of the last couple of days seemed to pass by like minutes. I needed this precious time to prepare for my nightly encounters. Was it just me? Checking the cylinder of my weapon for a full load, I spun the bullets randomly and slapped them hard inside the barrel. Normally I did such things for dramatic effect in the face of my adversaries, but I knew the enemy of this evening wouldn't be the slightest bit impressed. I breathed deeply as though the breaths were numbered bits of nourishment entering my body, preparing for the fight of its life. In many ways, they were. Tonight would be no different than last night or the night before. The fight of my life. Tomorrow night, I'd just repeat the process, I hoped. So on and so forth for all eternity, bout after unsuccessful bout, the dance with my former love Zoe was about to commence with the evening band's next song.

Glancing in all directions quickly, I sought out some type of shelter, weapon, or hiding place to use to my advantage. My luck returned right about that moment and offered nothing. Then again, who in the hell was I kidding? My luck had been nothing but bad since I first mounted Poon and headed for home. No sir, I was in the most desolate place imaginable. The pines were too far away, but I remembered what happened on the previous night among the trees and shook that idea off with a cringe. My cock thanked me. It was just me, the river, and the approaching doom formerly known as my wife. The least I could do for the bitch was make it as difficult as possible to get her clawed hands on my flesh one more time.

I entered the river with caution, but none of it seemed to matter. My feet whisked out from underneath me due to the current and slippery rocks, and I washed downstream at the mercy of the angry water. The rains from the sudden monsoon in the mountains had finally reached the valley, and she'd taken on more water than she knew what to do with. The river, I mean. She was flowing like synchronized menstruation at the saloon whorehouse. "Inventory week" is what some of the local boys called it, and I just chose to adopt the saying. Probably worth a slap across the face in some circles, but none of those prudes were around to lend a hand in my time of need. I'd heard one of them call my creative outbursts 'political incorrectness' at one time, but it all sounded like a bunch of made up nonsense. Must've been because I was in a church. I can imagine the Lord God Almighty, if there really is such a thing, doesn't like it too much when a sinful man enters his home and begins ranting about bleeding vaginas. Then again, that's what locks are made for. Don't just let strangers into your house if you can't stand impromptu, disgusting conversations. Political incorrectness? Yeah, politics worked well for President Lincoln a few months ago when someone replaced his brain with a bullet. The worst part of this whole scenario was that my brain was engaging in this line of thinking while helplessly washing down the goddamn Verde River.

I reached out for anything which could prevent my drowning, but the Mesquite trees and brush were too far from the banks to offer much aid. That's how incredibly desperate I was. I was willing to do a Jesus Christ on my hands with some Mesquite thistles to prevent myself from going any further down the river! 'Any port in a storm will do' is what the sailors in Boston would say when I was a child, but I imagined there wouldn't be much left of me after being washed through a grove of Mesquite trees, for sure! My whole body would probably look like something resembling my dick and I wasn't about to go there. At some point, if I lived through these repeated encounters with my unearthly princess Zoe, I'd like to be able to walk down the street in some town without children running for safety. It was bad enough my hand looked like it'd fisted a flaming hooker on a hot day. I didn't want the rest of my body catching up to make me appear all undesirable or anything. Filthy, snotty brats with their moral compasses and horror thresholds. I wonder what they'd do if I snuck up on them in a dark alley and rubbed this grubby, burned hand across their sweet little cheek? Scar those little bundles of joy for life, I truly would. I planned on making a mental note to do exactly that if I ever got out of this menstruating river.

Right about then, when I was having my twisted thoughts about ruining city folk kids, I slammed into a rock midstream. Granted, it prevented me from flowing any further down the Verde River, but it knocked the wind out of me as though I'd fallen flat on my back from a tall tree. I gasped for air to fill my lungs, but it was only being replaced with the cold, relentless water pinning me to my accidentally discovered, makeshift anchor. I attempted to climb a little higher out of the water, but the current kept pulling me back into the drink like it'd laid claim to my body with ownership rights. That bum, black hand of mine wasn't helping things too much, either. I could barely flex it without it cracking the flesh, resembling a swollen potato with five useless sausages attached. Still, I couldn't feel a thing from my wrist to my fingertips on that hand and was beginning to wonder if Zoe had put a skin walker mojo on it. I'm certain the snake bite wasn't helping much either but what can you do when you're being chased by a nightmare and your only choice for sanctuary is to voluntarily kill yourself in the Verde River? Hacking it off with the first toothy blade I came across buzzed around in my mind from time to time but then I wouldn't be able to scar the children. I guess I could ultimately hang onto it like a keepsake and do the same, but I don't think I had it in me to saw off an appendage. My poor penis wasn't even a stray thought in this conversation with blades and body parts. Peeled and split or not, I intended to hang onto that monstrosity until the bitter end.

Finally, my numb bare feet were able to find some imperfections in the rock and I climbed up to temporary safety. Almost to the point of freezing in the chilled night air of the desert, I stopped shivering long enough to see the disappointed face of Zoe Telos on the far bank of the river. Her inhumanly lengthy arms were stretched out hanging onto two pines while her scowl covered, pale face frowned in my direction. She looked slightly upset that the river hadn't finished me off, so I stood a little taller in a taunting manner. Deep down, I knew the wretched whore really didn't want me to die without her being the direct cause of the demise, so I began thinking of reasons for her to get on with the show. Burnt and snake bit hand, shredded dick, shivering Robert Jack had a few things to say before meeting his untimely death and exactly now seemed like the best time to get underneath her skin.

"Hey, old Zoe!" I began. "Fancy meeting you here! I thought that rotten fish smell was coming from the river until I looked over and saw you. Explains the whole thing now!"

Zoe looked somewhat upset with me, which I found unusual since I'd let her rape the skin off of my bone the night before without putting up much of a fight, and I couldn't quite put a finger—burnt to a crisp or otherwise—on it. Women tend to do that when you bring up the topic of undesirable scents flowing from their holiest of holies. If I recalled correctly, it always reminded me of the aftermath to a warm, springtime rain dripping down my beard and onto her stomach during those first few passion filled nights of love. Like I'd mentioned before, I waited until she was a reasonable age before I even went to such places so I'm not quite sure what the younger version of that would've been like. Probably smelled something like pee, I imagined, so I never even bothered asking the question of all questions before that time arrived. Yes sir, I was indeed a gentleman when it came to such encounters but that didn't mean I wasn't thinking about it. We'd snuggled for warmth and comfort for many years before I'd made her my bride and my dick had attempted to talk me into at least researching it a time or two. I'd just do what any other respectful man would do in those situations. Smack it hard a few times and tuck it down between my legs for safe keeping. After all, I didn't want the young beauty waking up to a situation which resembled a virginity robbing at gun point inuendo. No sir, warm spring rain and heaven's breath every time. Now? Sun baked fish on a riverbank mixed with remnants of the outhouse trough for sure! I clicked back the hammer on my Colt for good measure.

"Why, Robert Jack," she began with an unusual hint of the South in her voice. "Why would you say such a thing to your wife? You know this moist mess was more than good to you on a few occasions and you never seemed to be complaining about it then.

Why don't you just swim on over here and let me refresh your memory."

"Oh, you don't have to refresh my memory one bit, Zoe," I responded in a matter of fact manner. "I can't get last night out of my brain even if I took this here gun and splattered it all along the Verde River! On top of that, I'm not sure what's left of Little Robert Jack would appreciate any more of your moist mess in this life or what comes after. I'd ask him, but I'm afraid to look him in what remains of his eye. Why don't you swim your ghostly self out here so we can get this over with!"

Her scowl melted to anger, and she didn't hesitate to oblige my request. Slamming her almost transparent foot into the violent waters of the Verde, she pulled back in what appeared to be pain. Warm, visible vapors emanated from her saturated limb as though it disagreed with her entrance to the rushing fluid. She screeched with anger at her misfortune and immediately tried again for good measure. The result was identical. Something about the positive flow of the water was preventing the negative entity from crossing to my location, and I exhaled a sigh of relief. The good magic which remained in this ever changing, modernizing world had somehow given me a leg up in my fight against evil. Pondering what other cosmic wonderment I could discover in her presence, I jumped feet first back into the barrier waters of the Verde River and received the shock of a lifetime. My hand and crotch tingled with an otherworldly vibration. The charred mess formerly known as my disabled hand washed away into the nothing leaving behind fresh, new skin in its place. Without inspection, I imagined my cock was doing the same thing. Two good hands and a healed dick was sure to make my fight against her a little more even. Zoe's presence was the key to all harm I'd survived, and the same enigma was somehow responsible for my healing. To be honest, I looked down into my pants when I made it to the top of my sanctuary once again and smiled from ear to ear. The supernatural doorway, like all doorways, swung both ways when the veil was thin. I bet that Indian whore never thought I'd figure this out but indeed I did. Finally, I'd discovered a form of unusual protection from this Native curse on two legs, but I knew damn well I couldn't stay out on this rock forever. So did Zoe.

"You're just full of surprises, Robert Jack," she growled above the roar of the river. "Just imagine what else would be possible if you'd just give in to my desires. The two of us could be together forever like you promised. Unstoppable against anything the mere men of this world could throw at us. You and me, the way it was always meant to be! Come to me, Robert Jack, and I'll show you more than you could ever imagine."

"Oh, I can imagine quite a bit, Zoe girl," I chuckled. "If I ever voluntarily lay a hand on you again, it will be to discover a way to send you to Hell like I originally intended. That Indian whore might've found a way to prolong the inevitable, but she won't be around forever. I'm going to get you there, Zoe. You and that abomination of a child at the bottom of the well can share a room without my presence. I've never been much for the sound of screaming kids anyway. You deserve such torture and then some."

Zoe began to pace back and forth along the banks of the Verde River as though frustration was settling in. Occasionally, she'd dip a toe or two into the waters to see if nature's protection spell was nothing more than a fluke. Much to her disappointment, she jerked back each time as though she'd stepped on a thorny sticker in her own front lawn. I inhaled a cleansing breath, held it tight, and exhaled in a tribute to my current safety. She growled once more as she bore witness to my comfort. This obviously wasn't in her plan in spite of how tonight's festivities were supposed to transpire. Hell, if someone else had endured this lunacy, I wouldn't have believed them either. I probably would've bought them another drink to see how much further the maniacal story would go . . . but I never would've believed them. Honestly, I was living the whole thing and I was having trouble believing it myself. Too bad the newly found water mojo couldn't conjure me up a new set of boots to match my hand and dick!

"I'll get you, Robert Jack," Zoe threatened. "You're human and you need human sustenance. Granted, you have quite the unlimited water supply flowing all around your feet, but you'll get hungry at some point. You'll get hungry and come begging for me to cure your pain. When that time comes, I'll give you something to eat. You bet, Robert Jack. I'll give you something to eat that will take you over onto my side and we'll be together forever just like you promised."

For a second, I could've sworn I'd seen Zoe shed a tear as though a smidgen of sadness had entered her evil mind, but I could've been mistaken. Personally, I couldn't imagine that a freak such as her could feel any emotions like happiness or sadness. Not once had I witnessed her react when I mentioned the dead infant at the bottom of the well. No sir, it only seemed to upset her when she couldn't get her hands on me. It made me wonder how much sadness she'd possibly encountered during my absence from our home. After all, we'd been almost inseparable since our youth. Best friends who became lovers out of ultimate trust. I almost felt a slight sorrow for her myself, but noticed the aimed fire in her blackened eyes pointed directly at me and my rock. I was surely going to have to get over any emotions I still felt for this woman if I planned on surviving much longer. Whatever the two of us had together before I rode up on my cross-eyed horse a few nights ago no longer existed. She'd committed her sins and I'd committed mine. Me? My sins were all at the hands of a superior officer's orders. Hers? They were of her own choosing. No one forced her to go and share our bed with the likes of a Red Man or take a shot between her legs full of his native seed. No sir, she did those things on her own and there was no coming back from it. No making it right.

"Zoe Telos," I began my ultimatum. "I'd rather die out here on this lonely rock than ever ask you for anything ever again. Food or otherwise. If it all means I must get down to skin and bones out here on this rock, then so be it."

"You'll need me before it's all said and done," she responded with a hint of sadness. "What do you have on your side that could possibly keep you safe from my grasp, my power, and my will?"

Ultimately, she was right, and I knew it. Sure, the waters had performed their best to transform me back into something which resembled my former self before my whole world exploded somewhere in the vicinity of my own face, but I would indeed need food and other things at some point. I knew Zoe Telos wouldn't make the search for these items an easy task. Then, like a small, curious child peeking above the tall counter of a candy store, my temporary savior made its presence known on the Arizona horizon. I turned and smirked at her, pointing for what it was worth in an easterly direction.

"The sunrise," I answered, "I have the sunrise."

CHAPTER SIX
FRIDAY
END OF THE LINE

I **CHOSE NOT** to sleep when Zoe lumbered away to hide from the approaching sunrise. I didn't need to. Drinking from the river in her presence filled me with a renewed sense of strength the likes of which I hadn't felt since youth. It was as though its healing essence removed years of war from my body. I believed prolonged survival was once again obtainable even though I had no idea how it worked. I trusted my instincts, denying how illogical it all seemed.

I knew I needed to put as much distance as possible between me and Zoe Telos and the daylight hours were my only hope. The problem was that those particular hours were somehow sped up and under some kind of damn Indian skin walker voodoo. I wasn't quite sure what structure currently housed the beast, possibly an abandoned mine or cave, but I hoped it was in the opposite direction of my own intended sanctuary. I can only imagine she headed West to escape in the opposite direction of the coming morning, so I pointed my nose to the east. Besides, there was something I wanted to check out anyway. Zoe was right. I needed food to maintain my strength and continued safety. Food and potential weapons.

Yes sir, I was certain the Indian witch was correct. It would be damn near impossible to inflict harm upon something which can't be killed. I knew the flowing Verde River was somehow her nemesis, but I couldn't very well carry around a river in my pockets. The powerful, positive movement of the water did the trick but mere water itself wouldn't help at all. The rain sure as hell didn't offer any assistance while she was forcefully fucking me down to a nub. Yes sir! Skin walkers would be completely worthless in a rainstorm if that was indeed the case and I'm sure the powers that be in the other world wouldn't leave themselves open to such nonsense. Rivers, though? Few and far between in the Arizona/Navajo territory. I got lucky. I accepted it as merely that.

It wasn't long before my unfortunate bare feet came across some abandoned railroad tracks and my mind came alive with possibilities on a grand scale. If my internal map was correct, this line was abandoned at the beginning of the Yankee war so the workers could be utilized as bullet sponges. A lack of funding and materials had also been an issue since the money and metal was being used for cannon balls and bayonets. Still, the remnants of a railroad camp were possibly nearby. A potential cache of pickaxes, shovels, and supplies was only a couple of miles away from my current position. With any additional luck, maybe a few more guns, some ammo, and a pair of boots to protect my ever-deteriorating feet. Healing waters or not, they weren't doing too well and were the catalyst to my entire plan. In all fairness, it's kind of hard to run from your enemy without working feet. I picked up the pace to the best of my abilities.

It was still early morning by the looks of the sun's current position. Unlike previous days in which I'd slept away these precious hours, I had time to prepare for the evening's encounter. Absolutely, I knew for sure that Zoe's misfortunes from the night before would cause an anger within her the likes of which I'd yet to experience since her transformation. She'd been playing with me up to this point like an old Tom Cat with a cornered mouse. The only difference was that the cat never mounted the mouse and attempted to fuck it into oblivion. That would be a sight I'd hate to stumble upon but a hilarious one, nonetheless. Could you imagine it? Stumbling down the stairs at some ungodly hour of the night to inspect the racket and see the Tom just grinding away on this poor, helpless creature? I could imagine that the mouse's cock couldn't do much penetration on a Tom but there they are. Just fucking away in a corner while the mouse looks up at you, begging for assistance while Tom just wails into the darkness for all it was worth. What could you even do? Maybe crawl over to them on the grime covered floor and tickle their buttholes in hopes they finish quicker? I mean, if you take Tom away from the mouse and go back upstairs, they're just going to start fucking again right about the time you get comfortable. Might as well try to help them along for the sake of good times, right? I checked my own dick once more and returned from my trousers with satisfaction. Thank the maker for odd powers and rivers. I could finally piss straight again! If I got the chance, I would do it right into the face of my fallen foe the first time I got her onto her back all helpless like. Then again, maybe exposing my cock to that demon wasn't the best of ideas. I would just play it by ear and see how things went. If I got the chance, though, I totally planned on peeing in her face.

After a couple of hours of constant toe stubbing on the approaching railroad ties, I finally reached the remnants of the camp to find it abandoned. No sir, not another human being in sight. Weather worn tents flapped in the morning winds and not a particle of campfire smoke tingled my nose. Fortunately, the wooden cabins which held the explosives appeared to be intact and hopefully still held its precious contents for me to blow that bitch into oblivion. I immediately checked the remnants of Poon's saddlebags for a container of matches, but my personal luck reigned supreme yet again. I swear, I was destined to be without nice, normal things in my plight for survival, so I accepted it for what it was worth. I was indeed the world's worst at rubbing two sticks together. Maybe Christmas would come a couple of months early in this God forsaken desert and Santa would leave me a package full of boots, matches, and a rifle. It was a pleasant thought although highly unlikely. I was too far away from the Verde River now to even consider it to be any type of safety.

I entered the first of the sleeping tents with the caution of a mouse. Not the one getting raped by Old Tom, but the same kind you see scurrying here and there all over the desert floor. Scared little bastards. You know the type. Frightened of their own shadow, they are, and pissing all over your house and dropping scared little mouse turds all over the ground when you corner them. Those kind of mice, yes sir. I wasn't about to get tripped up by another predator looking for a meal or maybe water out here in the railroad camp. The workers appeared as though they were intelligent enough to take most of the worthy belongings along with them to whatever Hell hole they now occupied. Whatever military camp they now belonged to. Animals didn't know those things, though. They'd ravage this place from one corner to the other looking for a discarded slab of jerky or a water barrel still half full from the monsoons of the late summer and early autumn. Hell, the last thing I wanted to do was trip over a rattlesnake seeking shelter until the moon rose high in the sky. Personally, I'd had enough experiences with rattlesnakes to last me a lifetime as of late. My luck had already shown me a chance exists they'll bite your bad hand, turn into a preternatural whore, and grind your dick until there's nothing much left of it to even squirt with. No sir. Fuck those snakes dead off in their coiled-up arsholes was all I had to say about it. Fool me once, shame on the snake. Fool me twice? That could only be interpreted as me actually enjoying the crotch grinding I'd received from the poison pussy of Zoe Telos. I didn't like it at all. Maybe a few seconds here and there in the beginning, but not much toward the end.

As expected, I found nothing except two cots on top of empty foot lockers. No matches, no food, and no worn, stinky boots to protect these war-torn feet of mine. I laid atop one of the cots, the one which stunk the least, and closed my eyes for a second or two. I've been known to do some of my best thinking while on my back, not counting the molesting I'd taken in the pine forest. Something had to give between now and sundown or I was surely in for some abuse at the hands of my transformed wife. Goddamn Indian bitch and her mojo wasn't planning on making it any easier for me. No sir, not by a long shot. Hell, she's probably the one who came out here to the camp and stole everything for her own wellbeing. Probably killed and ate the poor lad who used to sleep on this cot, too! At least she would've eaten the one who smelled a bit nicer. The other one obviously belonged to someone who pissed and shite the bed all the time. Probably some silver miner who'd continued to sling that axe of his until well past his prime. Poor fellows had to make a living somehow, I guess. Slinging a blade by day and pissing all over himself by night. It was enough to keep the mountain lions and rattlers away. Yes sir! Absolutely a wonderful idea! Just cover myself in piss and turds until Zoe wouldn't want to have anything to do with me anymore! Then, I had a second thought, imagining having to smell myself all day baking in the desert sun, caked up with dried feces and such, and decided against it one hundred percent. It was at that exact moment when I got up out of the nicer smelling cot and got to work checking out the other tents.

My findings were similar no matter which tent I entered. Sure enough, I nearly tripped over one of those rattlesnakes as I entered the third tent, but I beat him senseless with Poon's saddle bag. Poor thing didn't even know what was going on and I kind of felt sorry for him. One second, he's the luckiest snake in the whole desert getting to hang out in the shade from the sun and tagging a defenseless, curious meal from time to time. The next moment passes and his damn brain is getting bashed in from a leather bag that used to belong to one of the most mentally challenged horses who'd ever galloped through the Arizona territory. Would've upset me more, if I was the snake of course, if I'd known that leather bag belonged to one with crossed eyes and got his dick caught between rocks. That would be my luck right about now as well. Old Robert Jack getting his head beat in by something which belonged to an animal who was so dumb, that he couldn't keep his own horse stick from dragging between two rocks. Inanimate objects for heaven's sake! In hindsight, it was no worse than getting your own peck grinded off by the same coot you used to stick your tongue in for fun and games. Made me shudder every single time I thought about it. Still, it didn't stop me. I bashed that snake into the ground for everything it was worth! You've got to teach those poor blokes a lesson, I thought. Beat him stupid so he can crawl back to the other rattlesnakes and tell them stories about the bad man with the leather bag. I'd be a legend in the world of those snakes, for certain. That's what they'll get, the slithering abominations. A visit from the Poon sack!

Rambling. Was I beginning to go crazy? All these random thoughts about ignorance in my head. Not that my mind was ever worth claiming in the first place, but it would be nice to keep it sane for just a bit longer. All this talk about cats humping mice and beating snakes with Poon's purse was making me wonder if some type of Indian witchcraft was to blame. Perhaps the loss of time I'd been experiencing was all in my head? Randomly blanking out with mental rants of insanity as the minutes floated on in my absence. I peeked my head out the tent for a quick look. Nothing moved except for a few tumbleweeds here and there. No Indian lady and, of course, no Zoe. The sun was still riding high in the sky from what I could tell. Then, the headache washed over me. I grasped my skull to hold it together. The tiniest of monsters was obviously trying to break free of my brain to enter this world. Not if I could help it, dammit! I could feel the skin atop my head crawl as though whatever newly formed nightmare inside my mind searched for a weakness. That was when the blackness overtook me.

Military madness occurred all around me, or at least that's what my noggin was telling me. I knew damn well I'd rode far away from that insanity on a horse named Poon not too terribly long ago and none of it could be real. It felt real, though. Cannon balls exploded all around me, spraying my comrades with grime and hot mess. I hunkered down for dear life inside the bowels of a hollowed-out Georgia Oak as blood caked the exterior bark. My nerves shook to insanity. I could barely see the outline of my own hands because they were shaking so fast. For a moment, it felt like both would break free from my wrists at any second! There he is, I thought to myself. There's the mighty Jacker, hunkering down in some Georgia Oak, scared out of his mind that the Yankees would take him and ram a sabre right up his arse. Wait. Was I watching this all unfold from outside my own body? I'd most certainly never witnessed anything like it. It was boring, really. Watching someone else's life play out for all to see? I wasn't quite sure what to call the experience, but I was sure there was a way to make a buck or two by charging admission. I'd have to remember this if I was ever able to hop back into my right mind. Moving pictures and such. Unthinkable nonsense as far as I was concerned. Hell, I would've gladly paid someone to remove me from the playback session. I didn't quite admire what I saw.

I was crying.

I remember that day all too well. All those years of bashing people's heads in with a pair of my own shoes, if that was all I had at my disposal, and no one other than myself knew how truly scared I was. Sure, I'd acted all tough for everyone else to see and, on more than one occasion, my shenanigans saved my hide. Fear is the ultimate controller when you live on the streets. Just then, with that thought, the playback switched to that of me as a young child, shivering in the Boston cold and at the mercy of anyone lucky enough to take advantage of the situation. The proverbial screen continued to flip in and out of my own life, only showing the times when I was truly frightened of the pathways laid before me. Honestly, it was most of them. I talked a mess of things when necessary, but I was really nothing more than the world's greatest actor. Just like those stage shows I'd encountered from time to time in the saloons on my way to the Arizona territory, it was all for show. My whole life was all for show. Suddenly, I noticed her.

I wanted to speak but wasn't quite sure what to

say. Old Zoe Telos sat there in all her teenage glory just like she was back when we first met on the streets of New York. She appeared to be watching the show the same as me but wasn't enduring the panic involved with revisiting her own life. No sir. She was watching the highlights of mine and the look on her face pretty much explained exactly what she thought of it all. I was nothing more than a coward with a small weapon and a big mouth. I put them both to good use out of desperation several times while growing up. She'd never even realized it until now. No, the girl had been too blinded by my reputation to know how much of a yellow bastard I truly was. In love with a faker. A fawney. Finally, she turned her head to speak in my direction. I braced myself for the scolding.

"You always thought you was the big dick in the street, Robert Jack, but you were nothing more than a tiny, scared little penis looking for a safe cunt to hide inside. That's what I became for you, Robert. I became your safe, little cunt . . . "

"Now be fair, Zoe Telos," I interrupted. "I never even took a crack at that crack until you were old enough to know better. You'd known me pretty long by the time I went spelunking in the Zoe hole . . . "

"Shut up!" she screamed furiously. Raising her right hand into the air and grasping her chair with the left, her previously undiscovered metaphysical powers came to life. A gush of air lifted my body into the nothing and swayed me back and forth with every motion she made. It was useless to move no matter how hard I tried. She aimed her eyes of fire directly into my soul.

STARVING ZOE

"This is all just a bad dream, Robert Jack. Any minute now, you're going to wake up in that stinky tent at the rail camp. You need to wake from this nightmare knowing two things. One? I know who you truly are and the cowardice you represent. I knew from the beginning you were nothing more than a liar and a fat mouth, but you were the liar and fat mouth I was in love with! I turned my head as you asserted your dominance over weaker creatures and people our whole relationship and pretended like you were the king overall. No sir, you were nothing of the sort. You were just the king of my world. My world! That was all that mattered. A king and his queen inside their tiny little desert cottage awaiting a couple of little princes and princesses. It's not too late to have that, Robert Jack. We could still have that."

I rolled my eyes with all my might since everything else on my body no longer worked. I wanted to make sure the dumb bitch saw them, too! There was no way I had any plans of making amends with someone who ground my dick to a stump with her rotting coot in the pine forests. She'd had her way with probably more than just the Indian, but he was the only one I truly knew for certain. I dropped his red baby into the bottom of the well. That was proof enough. Big fake or impressive son of a bitch, whichever I truly was in this God forsaken dream I called life, neither of those types of people deserved to put up with the broken trust of a true whore. That's exactly who Zoe Telos was at that moment. The truest of true whores. She was undead as well! Finally, Zoe noticed my continuous eye rolling and finished whatever lesson she'd planned on schooling me in.

"And number two?" I inquired sarcastically.

"Number two, Robert Jack?" Zoe giggled. "The number two lesson you need to walk away from this dream with is that I've kept you subconsciously occupied while the sun traversed its fateful journey to the West. Nightfall will be upon you soon and you'll be at my mercy once again. Just as a part of you is currently growing inside of me, a part of me is now growing inside of you as well. There's nothing you can do to stop it or get it out, either. You're going to love it, Robert. You'll see . . . "

With that, I snapped awake from the makeshift bed of dirt and rock I'd inadvertently landed on when I lost my bearings. The dream-devouring slut was telling the truth because only a sliver of sunlight could be seen between the wind-rustled flaps of the sleeping tent. The dizziness of the sudden headache had subsided, but Zoe's haunting last words worried me to the core. I didn't have much time to ponder the possibilities of what was inside of who, so I focused on the search for weapons instead. She'd be upon me soon for sure and I wasn't about to make it easy.

The all too recognizable echoes of Zoe's screech bounced among the nearby hills. Without a moment's hesitation, I ran for the explosives shed. I knew I hadn't located any matches yet but hoped to high heaven some idiot stored a box of them near the nitroglycerine cases. Honestly, who would do that? Who would be stupid enough to store a box of matches near the exploding death sticks that require matches to cause the death? It was the equivalent of a mouse building its nest on a feline farm. No wonder the mice were getting screwed by cats! They didn't have the sense not to bunk down near the kittens. Immediately, I shrugged the image out of my head, because it only led to deeper, more maniacal thoughts. There was no way I planned on having another black out episode like I did in the sleeping tent, so I tried my best to think happy thoughts. Well, more along the lines of thoughts which would ensure I'd see the light of another day.

Ramming the weight of my body into the door of the explosives shed time and time again, the barrier finally gave way to my desires. I chuckled aloud as the disappearing sunlight revealed the box of matches sitting atop a half empty crate of explosives. The bad part of my luck set in after the sudden victory as no detonators were readily available. The plan I'd formulated in the beginning was to just set the whole shed on fire anyway, so it mattered none. No sir! Not at all! Just take one of those matches, torch the building, and run like Hell once Zoe got close. I reached deep within the crate hoping to locate one that hadn't been rain soaked from the shotty seal job and, much to my surprise, found something entirely different. It was long and slender, like nitro but with a fuse already shoved down inside of it. Two words decorated the outside.

Nobel.

And *Dynamite.*

A funny name for a guy who likes to blow things up if you ask me, but I was damned proud of Mister or Missus Nobel Dynamite. If the theory rattling around in my head was indeed true, I wouldn't need to blow up the whole shed at all. I could just light it and throw it at the bitch! Thank you very much,

Mister or Missus Nobel Dynamite! If it was entirely up to me, I would've given them some kind of prize . . . or at least a drink at the saloon if I ever again regained my peace. The 'Dynamite Peace Prize' had a nice ring to it, for certain!

Double checking the crate, I surely had the only stick not saturated from the earlier monsoons. Fate, you could call it, that this one, single section of God-knows-what survived in that open crate but who was I to look a cross-eyed gift horse in the mouth? I knew damned well that statement didn't make a lick of sense because I paid for Poon fair and square. That sly Australian didn't put the four-legged abomination in gift wrap for me. No sir! I truly had no idea what this little stick of The Savior's goodness had in store for me and Zoe, but I was more than willing to try it out. That was right about the time a pale, clawed hand I knew all too well rested atop my right shoulder. I didn't even need to turn around. I just needed to stall her.

"We meet again, Robert Jack!" Zoe's scratchy voice bellowed. "You won't be able to wish away this encounter by merely waking up and there's no rushing river to lend you aid."

Old Zoe surely had me dead to rights, and I had to think quick if I planned on seeing the dawn. I dared not flinch to reveal the plan being hatched in my mind, so I just stood there staring at the far wall of the explosives shed. Hopefully she'd have the good will not to slash me from neck to butt crack while my back was turned. If I could keep her talking about useless topics, maybe the other worldly twat would grant me the moment I'd need to send her rapist coot into oblivion. Then again, if there was anything the great Robert Jack was good at, it was indeed talking about useless topics!

"Why'd you play me out to be some kind of coward in my dreams, Zoe?" I spoke over my shoulder, never allowing her to see my eyes. "You know damned well I saved your life on the streets of New York more times than you're willing to admit! It wasn't fair to make me see myself that way. No ma'am, not at all. Made me begin to doubt myself in my own dreams. Almost shed a tear a time or two if you must know. I know better, though. I know who I am, Zoe Telos. I'm still 'The Jacker', and I don't have to be gutting rich lads and cops in alleyways to prove it to anyone. Especially you. I've survived my childhood, conquered this desert, and outlived the war against the Yankees. I'll survive you, too!"

She paused in her retort, which was unfortunate. I was hoping to use the sounds of her God-awful voice to mask the noises of me tinkering around with the matches. On top of that, I still hadn't the slightest clue about the chaos this little stick of Nobel would cause once I lit it up. For all I knew, the fuse on this son of a bitch would burn so fast that I wouldn't have a chance to do much other than blow us both to the moon! I imagined for a second what that would look like and smiled with temporary happiness. Zoe flying up through the sky and banging her ugly face into that glowing orb. Just a black shadow on its shining surface from now until the end of time, reminding all other cheating witches what might happen to them if they don't straighten up and fly right by their husbands. This was 1865, by God! No need for any of that cave woman behavior by running around and swallowing every single swinging dick they encountered. Yes sir, indeed! No need in acting like a blind whore in a cornfield. It just wasn't civilized frontier behavior.

"I'll make you a deal, Robert Jack," she whispered into my ear as tenderly as a dead bitch could. "You lay with me in this shed one last time and I'll grant you every ounce of your freedom from my grasp. Love me like the woman I once was, and this will all end tonight."

It wasn't even remotely tempting. Not only did my mind turn to immediate flashbacks of Zoe grinding my helpless nub into the nether realm, but it damned near turned my most prized possession inside out. If there was any such thing as a negative erection, then I was truly experiencing one. The dangler was probably hanging out of my own arshole like the turd that refused to taper! I cleared my throat to attempt my greatest con to date.

"You bet, sweet Zoe," I replied with false sincerity. "I remember how much you loved me, and I'd want nothing more than to feel that love one last time. Yes, I'll lay with you in this here shed."

I didn't believe for a minute that the bitch took the bait until she brushed past me. Sensually, or as sensually as the decomposing remnants of a woman could be, Zoe straddled the floor on all fours as though I meant to climb in behind her and give it the old what for. The lips of what remained of her pussy separated slowly with a tiny smack of moisture bringing the stench of death directly into both my nostrils. I held my breath to prevent gagging. I was sure that vomiting hadn't become a type of aphrodisiac, but I wasn't about to gamble with my chances. When I was a teenage boy experimenting with all the ladies of the night, not once did one of them give me a price for vomiting on them. Now that I'm mentioning it, none of them had a foot in the coffin either. It was at this point in my skewed thought process when I decided to let fate take its course in the tiny explosives shed after all. Zoe glanced back at me with ecstasy in her eyes as I struck the match, lit Nobel Dynamite's fake dick, and slammed it as far inside Zoe's cunt as I possibly could. Yes sir, it's a little difficult getting up off your knees in a cramped space. Even harder removing a flaming explosive from your puss with clawed hands.

I managed to get a good hundred feet away before the explosion took me off my own legs. The tiny hut splintered the desert surroundings as what I thought to be a dozen or so more useless sticks of explosives went up right along with it. I can imagine the surprise that went through her mind as that blast in the arse she begged for became the last blast she'd ever receive. It was brilliant, and it was finally over. At least I believed it was for the moment. Sure, she'd be back, but she'd be whistling while she walked!

CHAPTER SEVEN
SATURDAY
CALL TO ARMS

AT SOME POINT during my flight from the explosion and possibly the most pissed off skin walker who'd ever walked in a skin, my brain went into overdrive. I needed to fill up on every necessity known to man and I knew exactly where to get it. At least, I hoped I did. The volunteer fort was directly to the South of my current location. The tracks from the camp led straight there. They didn't go far in the other direction, but they sure enough led to the fort. A part of the Confederate military plan which fell through at the very last second. It's a little difficult to transport your troops by train if the tracks don't lead you straight to the frontlines of the war.

I remembered the fort all too well from when I was first commanded to enter the service of the Confederate Army to fight off the Yanks. Goddamn place didn't even have a name. I was basically handed a gun and wished good luck. At some point, these military soldiers need to start training these poor kids who might very well one day mirror my predicament.

STARVING ZOE

I'm not going to lie one bit. No sir! I could've used some of that training while dodging the bullets and blood from the Northern aggression! That's what we'll call it. Northern aggression. Makes it sound so much more civilized than kicking a Yankee in the balls, especially since us boys in gray were the ones who were on the receiving end of the ball kicking. Let's not split hairs, though. We called it a draw, but I'm certain the history books will say otherwise. At least we got to keep the South. Better weather in the grand scheme of things. Nicer women, too! All except mine, who should be making her way back from the moon at any moment.

The morning sun rose once more in my favor, and I knew I had enough time to get the essentials under control. Food, footwear, and firepower. Sure, it was going to be a tough sell to the soldiers on duty out at the fort, but I could con the devil into a glass of ice water were it truly necessary. The truth would be a little much for their sensitive ears, but I'm sure they'd believe me. I used to be one of them, after all. Absolutely! Just tell them all that I tried to kill my wife for dabbling in the color red, or the other way around, and some Navajo bitch turned her into a freak of nature. What's not to believe about that? Indians were always up to nonsense and that's why the military was kicking their red tails out of Arizona and into the New Mexico territory. They both looked identical, to be real about it all, so I really didn't see what all the fuss was about. Roll up your teepee and get on with life! Yes, I know it was cruel to think of a fellow human being treated that way, ignoring their skin color, but I felt as though I'd been wronged by the entire race! Never had a bad thing to say about any of those Indians until one of them moved in my house, messed up my fit, and left a crying half-breed kid in my own bedroom. Surely that was more than enough reason for a little good, old-fashioned hatred! I knew good and well that one of those savages would put an arrow right through my head if given the chance. They wouldn't even have to know about me throwing one of their tiny kin folk into a well full of rattlers. No sir, they'd just tag me one right through the ears for the simple fact I was a white man. I mean, it was 1865. What had we done to deserve such treatment? Where did those Indians get the idea to repress an entire race of people?

I was rambling in my head again. I shook it to get any thoughts out not pertaining to the essentials. It damn sure was a hard thing to do in my situation. I'd met nothing but crazy since I first dismounted that cross-eyed horse. Things like that tend to screw up your mind, you know what I mean? How in the hell would one expect to stay sane with a lifestyle such as mine? No, it wasn't all bad. Not all the time. From war-torn to whore-scorn, I think I deserved a little crazy stray thought every now and then. The only problem was that they were coming more and more often. More so since I'd been back in the presence of Zoe Telos.

It was like my brain's train jumped the tracks somewhere along the lines of finding that kid and then tying her to that Mesquite tree along the Verde River. I was also sure that the Navajo witch had something to do with it, too. They had the power to get inside my skull at the most inopportune times!

Starving Zoe

Maybe that's what Zoe did during the daylight hours since her ugly skin couldn't touch the light. Just sit back in some dingy cave and use those supernatural perks of hers to intrude inside my noggin. Would I even be able to stop her from doing so once I'd filled her full of lead? Hell, for that matter, would I even be able to kill her? I guess the master plan was to keep shooting her until I found out. The problem was I kept forgetting about this Colt Army on my belt whenever she showed up. Was I frightened beyond remembering or ultimately scared to send my wife to her grave? The mean gent inside my head likes to talk tough. Sometimes it loses something in the translation between my brain and fingers.

The front gates to the fort were littered with Indian arrows. What the red devils hadn't skewered was burned to piles of ashes sporadically between the high walls. As the cold, October wind blew clouds of what remained of the destruction into my face, I couldn't help but feel a bit defeated. Sure, this had nothing to do with me personally but, dammit, when in Hell's happy hollows was I going to receive a well-needed break? All the elements seemed to be against me at once and I flipped my middle finger into the breeze for absolutely no one to see. Just exactly who was I flipping off? The distant mountains? The ghosts of the poor suckers who had the nerve to stand and fight the Navajo who raided this place into oblivion? Only two structures remained intact. At least it appeared as such from the outside. For all I knew the insides of those buildings could've been torched to pieces and I, yet again, would be out of luck. With only a few hours until sunset, I knew it was high time I checked out the situation rather than ponder the possibilities.

One of the remaining structures was definitely a church. That much I knew for certain. The giant cross on top of the steeple was a dead giveaway. Not saying that I don't believe in the powers of the good Lord but who in this world didn't know a church when they saw one? Did it need to be advertised so damn much all the time? I ranked it right up there with a door to door catalog salesman. I mean, who in this world isn't wiping their own back side with this catalog and who doesn't have one in their outhouse in the back? You read the page, then you use it to smear the nastiness off, right? Do we really need some son of a bitch going door to door to tell you about the catalog? The answer is no. I don't need someone knocking on my front door at inconvenient times of the day trying to clue me in on the existence of mail order catalogs. I know it. My arse knows it. Get on with life, you worthless peddlers of the mail order industry! Churches, though. Same stuff, different format. There are crosses all over the buildings, Bibles, and bitches' necks. They're always trying to shove it in your face like we have no idea what they are. Now, if I was an idiot, and it's open to debate, I could see where getting the two confused could land you in the naughtiest of naughty places. Certainly, someone out there has messed up a time or two and accidentally wiped himself with the Bible rather than a mail order catalog. "Thou shalt not wipe thyself on the pages of the good book," is the unspoken Eleventh Commandment right behind "don't use the pages of this book to roll up your wacky weed," and "please

STARVING ZOE

tuck me into the bedside drawer if you plan on fucking the saloon whore." Pure poetry in motion. I can imagine the Hell you'd have to pay if you popped it out of her well-oiled cooter and sprayed your load all over the Book of Matthew. This guy begat that guy and then that guy begat an umbrella. No sir. I had enough to deal with in my day to day life without bringing the wrath of the creator upon me for sprinkling a batch of my little Bobbies and Betties atop his sacred word. Needless to say, I intended on skipping the investigation of the chapel out of aversion for thinking about jerking off in the presence of God. You must know when to bow your head in penance and when to tuck your dick back into your trousers. Never get those two mixed up and always do them in that order. If you bowed your head before tucking your dick, there's a chance of shooting yourself in the face. Dangerous ground, I tell you. Dangerous ground.

I entered the remaining structure with the only ounce of hope in this weathered heart of mine, and it paid off. A row of beds and footlockers, which appeared to be untouched by the flames and Indian onslaught, showed itself to me in a display of grandeur! It was indeed time for pilfering through other people's belongings in hopes of getting a leg up on sweet Zoe's nightly arrival. I decided to start near the back of the room first, so I'd be advancing toward the door as time went by. The last thing I needed was to get caught in a room full of beds when the time came. Old Zoe's puss seemed to have it in for me, and an encounter in a room full of bunks would've given her way too many options. Then again, that pussy of hers had gotten the blast of a lifetime the night before and she might not be up for any play just yet. Yes sir! You probably could drive a team of horses through that crack after what I did to it with that stick of Nobel. Slip her on like a knee-high boot, I was certain. You'd even have enough room to wiggle your toes around for the pleasure of it all! Blasted one big hole between her coot and butt to where it resembled a kiddie sock puppet show whenever she walked! Poor bitch. The next soul she fell in love with would be able to fist her on like a gauntlet and work her like a circus ventriloquist.

The farthest footlocker within the bunk house was stenciled with the name of Liberman. Digging through his most valuable possessions, I found a book with a bunch of funny writing I didn't understand hidden beneath a worn pair of boots that were just my size. I flipped through it a bit while lacing up my feet's saviors but couldn't quite get a grasp on any of the symbols. I'd heard stories about people other than the Indians who believed differently from the Christian-type folk in this country but never met one face to face . . . or at least one that admitted to believing differently. Maybe that was it, though. Maybe he was scared to be honest and felt like he needed to hide it all beneath this pair of stinky boots. I mean, if I wasn't in dire need of foot protection, I never would've moved these wretched things to discover his book. I'd recalled stories from the other Irish immigrants back in Boston about the witches who'd dance naked in the moonlight while worshipping a goddess who dated back further than God, Jesus, and everyone else mentioned in the Bible. Most of them were burned alive when found out, so maybe this fellow felt the same way.

It's funny how someone or something meant to bless lives always associated himself or itself with so much death and destruction. Bothered me sometimes. Seriously, I would lay awake at night and think about it all the time when I was growing up on the streets. So many put faith in that ancient book we pray over, but those same people refused to think outside the box for apprehension of what they might discover. I, for one, needed all the help I could get throughout this life and never wanted God to find out I was looking over his shoulder. I guess I was no different than this Liberman fellow. Hiding my own version of the good book behind the stinky boots of my soul for avoidance of what others thought. I'd learned differently over the past week. I don't remember anything in the Christian Bible about scorned bitches coming back to life and Navajo skin walkers. Maybe it's time for society to write a new chapter in that book to update the folks in the here and now on how to live and treat each other. Whether you believed in what your neighbors thought outright, danced naked in the woods, or read books composed of unusual letters, no one deserved to live in dismay or be burned alive. I covered the book with a few of his shirts just in case he was still alive somewhere out there in the Arizona wilderness. I didn't want the wrong gent to find it. It was the least I could do for the boots.

Second came a footlocker stenciled with the name of Ravenwood near the middle of the room. It was filled to the brim with the same type of religious whatnots I'd been discussing at the previous trunk, and I chuckled out loud at the thought of these two guys sleeping in close proximity of one another. I wondered if they even knew. No sir, this Ravenwood guy was obviously the fort's priest or a pack rat for the holier things in life. Not being too particular or trying to play favorites in a room full of choices, I praised any and all gods when I moved a torn pair of pants to discover a sealed container of preserved jerky. I tore into it like a coyote to a fallen deer and give a little nod to the God I'd grown up with for looking out for me.

See what I mean there? You can talk madness all day long about what you believe in or what you'd like to believe in, but it all comes down to what's been drilled into your head when the chips are down. Then again, it could've all just been a spot of convenient luck and my brain just translated it into a blessing. I pondered that fine line between tastes of the heavenly, dried meat when the glimmers of sunlight of the closing day caused a sparkle to catch my eye. Wadded up in the furthest corner of Ravenwood's footlocker was a silver St. Christopher's necklace. My first instinct was to grab it out of pure value, but I stayed my hand for karma's sake. I nodded again in quick prayer in hopes the trinket would someday find its owner and closed the locker's lid for additional safe keeping. I was probably going to need God's help before this night was over and it wouldn't have been in my best interest to piss him off at the last second. I'd already risked it with all the stray thoughts stirred up by Liberman's weird little book. I apologized with a whisper to the invisible god of my upbringing and moved to the last bed. That was when I heard the screech of Zoe on approach. Once again, I'd lingered too long within my own head and lost track of time!

I shivered in my newly obtained boots and flipped the lid to a footlocker stenciled with the name of Burns. Whatever had been inside of this case had been torched to ashes the same as the other buildings on the grounds of the fort. There was nothing. Absolutely nothing. No sir. Whoever this intelligent fellow was decided to take all their belongings with them when they left for greener pastures or burned it to keep people like me from rummaging through it. I didn't blame them one bit. Between the Indians patrolling this desert and the skin walker problem, I could see why anyone wouldn't want to stay put for too long. I took the clue and bolted for the only other building still standing in the wake of the fort's disaster.

It was too late to try and secure the fort's front gates, but I tried my damnedest. Pushing with all my might, the boots just couldn't get the grip on the ground needed to budge the large, wooden barriers. I looked down to reveal them slipping into large puddles of blood in the sand that reflected the rising moonlight. No matter how hard I pushed, pulled, and kicked the things, they refused to move and were probably the direct cause of the fort's demise to begin with. Surely, I imagined, Liberman, Ravenwood, and Burns probably stood in the exact same spot as me kicking and cussing for all it was worth when the Indians rode over the hill flicking flaming arrows at the wood. Not one of them gave a damn about the differences in their religion at that exact moment and prayed to the same heaven, just translated into different languages, as the Navajo offered their scalps to the third god they'd brought into the mix. Fear and loathing for this miserable life as the sharpened stones of their tomahawks pierced the brows of those men's heads, spilling their essence onto the ground of this cruel desert.

I mean, where were all the soldiers? I came here for supplies, absolutely, but I was hoping deep down there would be a gaggle of government paid goons here to help me ward off my unnatural princess. There was blood at the front gates but no bodies! If there was a slaughter here, it was entirely minimal. They probably all headed down South to the silver mines springing up all over the place to get rich quick. Personally, I had no business down there whatsoever. Mining is harder work than I'm willing to do of my own free will and the food makes me fart uncontrollably. Staining my britches in front of pretty women due to a slight cough was not worth its weight in precious metals. There was nothing but wall to wall swinging dicks at this place when I was first enlisted into the Army and I literally mean swinging dicks! A line of men who'd been obviously more gifted than I was during the birthing process wound in and out between the buildings waiting to see some doctor. What in the wide world of weenies was this man looking for anyway? What can you tell about a man by looking at his cock? Basically, all you can do is stare it in the eye and say, "yep, that's a dick alright"! Did anyone bother to check this man's credentials or his medical certificate? I personally never believed he was a doctor at all. No sir, not at all. Probably just some drifter who got off on looking at dicks all up close and personal. Not once did I ever meet a doctor who just wanted to jingle my jewels for medical purposes. On top of that, what would the verdict be if something unusual was discovered? "Sorry, son, but I can't let you go fight the enemy today. Your dick is looking a tad subpar." Idiocy! Pure idiocy! You bet! Just an old drifter who wandered into camp with a white coat, putting one guy's cock into his mouth after another saying, "tastes fine to me. Next." I'd never make it in medical school, for sure!

My seconds were ticking away, and I gave up all efforts with the gates to head for the ironic safety of the chapel. I tried with all my might to keep my balance during flight but rolled to the ground a couple of times here and there. I'm certain Zoe was getting a slight kick out of me falling on my face as I fled, and I made myself a mental note to ask her whenever she arrived to kill me. Sure, that was the way to delay the inevitable during the night's confrontation. Keep her confused with small talk, I thought. She'd love it. Then again, the back of my mind was chock full of thoughts about how pissed off she probably was concerning me fucking her with a stick of explosives and blowing her to smithereens. I couldn't help but feel tonight would be all about blood and less about my wit. She would slaughter me for certain if given the chance now and, in a way, I guess I'd earned it.

I could've just as easily woken her on the night of my arrival to conversate about loneliness, babies, and stray Indian dick, but it didn't feel like the right thing to do at the time. Kill the baby, leave the bitch for dead, and move on with my life. Yes sir! It's exactly what any other man in my position would've done if he'd returned home to discover the mayhem I did. Well, any man with a set of balls, that is. I'm sure there are a few of them out there whose wife kept their testicles in a preciously carved box on the fireplace mantle who'd just accepted things for what they were, but not this man. No way! I reached for my pistol mid run and popped off a couple of rounds over my shoulder for good measure. After all, it felt like the bitch was breathing on the back of my neck and I didn't want to turn around again to see. Yep, just shot off a couple of bullets for good measure in the general direction of her approach. I never planned on hitting her, you see, I just wanted the cunt to know I was still in the game and ready to play overlooking the fact I was sure to lose. As expected, I either didn't hit her or they did little damage upon impact. Zoe howled right back at me to let me know she was still coming.

I reached the front porch steps to the chapel and grabbed onto the bannister for all it was worth. The arrival at the holy structure didn't do much for my worn nerves but I expected that when I first chose to make my final stand on its hallowed ground. My labored breath heaved in and out of my lungs like it mattered. It didn't. Each inhale was accompanied by a sear of pain as though I'd accidentally swallowed a concoction of fire and thorns. The blur in my eyes finally began to disappear as my breathing slowed. I stared into the eternal darkness of the desert night expecting to see the pale, slender body of Zoe appear through the veil.

Emptiness filled my ears as the creatures of the night took their vow of silence in the presence of the master predator. She'd yet to show her face but I knew she was there. I could hear her breathing. I could feel her anger toward me wafting on the air like it was a tangible warning of her arrival. I hunched down in the doorway in hopes that the blackness contained within the walls would be enough to mask my location. Old Zoe would know that the last place I'd choose to be seen would be within the walls of a church and, with any luck, she'd fail to look for me there. That was the plan for sure! I would just take off running in the opposite direction while she tore apart the bunks in the barracks looking for me. A hidden clock within the sanctuary chimed seven strokes in the darkness revealing to me the exact time of my nearing demise. Whether or not this clock had been wound to exact precision or even if the master of the timepiece had the good sense to set it rightly was none of my concern at the moment, so I believed with all my heart that it was indeed seven o'clock. That was right about the time I felt a clawed hand tear through the flesh of my shoulder along with the realization this church had a previously unknown back door. Zoe knew about the back door, for sure. She'd chosen to use it rather than come face to face. Lucky me. A dull pain across the back of my head was the last thing I remember on the final 'normal' Saturday of the life I'd come to know. The light inside my head joined with the darkness which already surrounded me. I was out.

CHAPTER EIGHT
SUNDAY
CLOSER TO GOD

I WAS FADING in and out of my own reality when the clock decided to strike up another mystery conversation. Twelve chimes I counted as my vision began working properly to reveal someone looking over me that I wasn't too interested in viewing. Investigating my surroundings, it was revealed that my arms and legs were tied to a damned life-sized cross above the pulpit just like that Jesus Christ fellow in the Bible. The real Jesus who belonged on this thing was laying on the floor below me in a childlike fetal position. Not the 'real' Jesus, mind you, but a wooden carving of the dude just discarded on the ground by the crazy crone decorating my field of vision. Not once in my life had I ever put two and two together to realize what Jesus would look like if you took him off the cross and threw him on the floor. He looked downright frightened, he did. Almost like he'd had a bad run in with that doctor man who used to work here. The absolute victim of a cock tasting gone horribly wrong. Way too much kneeling involved in religion. Eventually, that sort of deal was bound to happen. Getting on your knees in front of other men tends to put you at a convenient dick height for anyone with ill intentions. Fool me once? Shame on you. Fool me twice? Chances are you weren't fooling me at all, and I was just seeing if you were fit for military service.

"I'm so glad you've decided to join me in my time of utmost need, you raggedy Indian bitch," I initiated the conversation with my solo spectator. "It's funny how you always seem to show your scraggly mug at the most convenient times. I can image all you do is just sit your chunky rump on a mountain top, gnawing on whatever unfortunate critter happens your way, waiting on Zoe to send up a smoke signal for you to waddle over and make my life difficult!"

The red-faced whore cracked a broken smile resembling the worst carved pumpkin in Samhain's history. I had every intention of bringing that fact to her attention, but I knew damned good and well that it referenced a holiday unknown inside her feeble mind. The Irish immigrants in Boston and New York celebrated it faithfully when they came here but it scared the living hell out of everyone else, especially the Christian church folk. Believed it weakened the walls between the world of the living and the haven of the dead. Like a beacon for all the bad things to come pouring into this world and raise a ruckus. What they failed to realize was that all bad things pour themselves into this world even without a lantern to signal the way. Regardless, this tuckered out taint still wouldn't get the reference, so I refused to waste the time it would take to explain. Still, the slut had a smile like a cemetery that'd had half of its markers kicked over. Finally, she hid her broken teeth behind her crusted lips and began to speak whatever sage wisdom she'd planned on sharing.

"Oh, Robert Jack," she began. "I wouldn't have missed this for the world. To see you up there strapped to that wooden cross just like that martyr the white men all preach about. Pure heaven. Not their hard-candy-coated version of heaven that their mommies and daddies all promised them at bedtime to keep the boogie men away, but my personal idea of heaven. The kind that sees you lingering on the edge of death and making everything right once more."

Sure enough, that bitch had tied me up nice and proper, because I couldn't move an inch in either direction. I wanted nothing more than to hop off this cross and slap what remained of her dental nightmare across the floor of the church. Just watch them scatter beneath the pews like a loaded set of dice on a saloon craps table. I imagined her dropping down to gather her cracked molars to realize she'd rolled a set of snake eyes. The laughter came on suddenly and it took her by surprise. Almost as though she was having difficulty understanding why someone in my current predicament would laugh so heartily. At that moment, I decided my best course of action would be to keep her talking. Perhaps it would grant me the moments to find a flaw in her rope tying abilities.

"Look lady, I don't even know what I'm supposed to call you. If you have every intention of killing me, don't you think it's fair for me to know the name of the great harbinger of death who bested The Jacker? Indeed, you have bested me because I'm stuck up here on this cross for you to do whatever you see fit for throwing your grandchild down a well. Personally, I think it's only fair."

She began to pace back and forth as though she'd entered deep thought, picking apart the existence of her own name. Surely, I wasn't the first gentleman who'd ever asked. I mean, I thought I'd known enough about the Indians over the last few years of my life to understand they indeed had names. They were all interesting bits pertaining to actions and animals and whatnot. Kicking Coyote or Incontinent Owl. Never once was it a Tom, Dick, or Harry like when you met a white person in the street of a civilized town. No sir. It was always something like Fiery Fox or Constipated Crow. Maybe I'm offering up the wrong examples, but you get the general idea of what I'm saying. Made up nonsense, you know? Then again, maybe names didn't mean all that much to any of those painted up sons of bitches and that was what we seemed to be dealing with as I was tied up to this cross. Maybe no one had ever given her a name. It was at this exact moment when I decided to grant one to her obviously confused psyche. Just a little nudge in the right direction.

"Never mind, I'll just call you Hillary," I offered. "I knew this one-eyed hooker back in Brooklyn whose mid-section smelled like a whole hot wad of dammit but you could still get the job done if you held your breath long enough. Halitosis Hoo Haa Hillary is what we used to call her. Not to her face, mind you. I mean, it's one thing to be a paid whore but paid whores have feelings too! We mostly just called her Hillary to her face. To her crotch? Well, that was a different story altogether. It literally smelled as though someone went down there a time or two and vomited inside her puss. Almost like you'd spit out a mouthful of peas and carrots when you came up from repaying the favor on her. It'd be a little hard to do that to someone and then have to look them in the face. Especially when they only have one eye. Kind of narrows down your choices, doesn't it?"

She flinched at my tale which, to me, was an obvious sign she'd accepted the designation. Yes sir! Hillary it was. Perhaps this would be the ice breaker between the two of us I'd been inadvertently looking for. One could hope, so I did. Unfortunately, she began to walk toward the front doors of the chapel.

"Oh, come on, Hillary, where are you going?" I begged the question. "It really felt like we were making progress. Won't you stay and chat with me a bit longer? We're just getting to know each other!"

She turned on me like a pissed off hedgehog, all bristled up and ready for trouble. Now, I wouldn't expect her to know what a hedgehog was since she was all primitive, but I'd seen one in a traveling show once. Little prickly things came from Africa or Australia or one of those other countries I have no interest in visiting. The barker kept nudging me to pet the evil little creature as though it was a domesticated house pet and I received a handful of spikes. I beat that man about the face with my already bleeding hand making his head look much worse than what it was, but I guarantee you he never asked anyone else to pet that little devil in disguise ever again. Anyway, Hillary Hedgehog was getting all tense on me and pointing her bony finger toward my face all matter-of-factly. I hated fingers to my face, but I listened without much argument on my part for once. Maybe she had something important to say after all?

"I'm done with you, Robert Jack," Hillary answered. "I'll have no more dealings with your troubled soul from this moment forward. You're Zoe's problem now. I pray she deals with you properly. Make the right choice, Robert Jack. When the time comes, make the right choice."

With that, she turned one final time and was gone from my world. Good riddance, I thought to myself. Unfortunately, it took her a long time to get out the door due to a trail of fat waddling behind her. Yes sir. A good ten feet of red arse followed behind her like one of those cabooses at the end of a slow steam train. I half expected some poor bastard to be hanging off the end of it waving a lantern. I'd never seen an Indian bitch with so much arse before. Must've been a nice life she'd had lounging around in the chairs of my home never having to lift a finger. Quite a bit of a lifestyle change from having to be like those other Navajos dodging soldiers' bullets and hunting for food. For sure, she just sat there under my roof while I was fighting in the war being fed like a trained animal. Just lazily watching the world go by outside my living room windows until something better came along. Absolutely! Good riddance to Hillary, her arse, and the little man waving the lantern on her caboose. At least she wasn't around to see my right hand come free from the ropes of the Jesus cross. That was about the time Zoe stuck her ugly mug inside the chapel doors.

"You didn't have to be so mean to her . . . "

C. Derick Miller

I shut that whore up mid growl all nice and proper with a shot to her saggy, decomposing tits! It must've taken her totally by surprise because she stumbled backward a bit. Holding the bleeding boob in the palm of her hands like a coddled child, she grazed her fingers atop the bullet wound like it made a difference. Taking full advantage of the distraction, I put a bullet through the three remaining ropes and dropped to my knees for a full on reload of my revolver. This was right about the time when she stopped staring at her wounded breast and put full attention onto me.

Charging in my direction, she knocked the pews over one by one with extended, clawed hands. A fierce stare of vengeance pierced my soul and I felt it all the way down into my newly booted feet. Well, they were new to me anyways. That Liberman fellow had made sure to get quite a bit of use out of them and the soles were damn near worn down to nothing, but it was better than going barefoot with all the bits of chaos flying around this church. I hammered off six more shots into Zoe's mid-section as she neared my location. She stumbled backward again, losing balance, and landed on her dead, skin walker back side with a thud. I did the only other sensible thing a man in my position of disadvantage would do at a time like this. I brought old Jesus Christ into the fight!

I picked up Mister Jesus with his newly found purpose and rammed him headfirst into the face of Zoe. Repeatedly, I smashed the savior into her skull as the blood began to fly throughout the chapel. I was good and pissed off, I was, otherwise I'd never have thought about picking up a wooden carving of Jesus

Starving Zoe

Christ and beating my wife about the face. You do things, bad things, in the heat of the moment all the time when you're a man and there's hardly never an explanation for any of it. Today was different, though. Today, I smashed that bitch with a true purpose! That purpose was indeed the continuation of my own miserable little life past sunrise. Sure, it was only nearing the one o'clock hour on this fine Sunday morning, and I had a few hours to go until the sun reared its head above the horizon, but no one planned on attending this church when that happened. Yes sir! They'd all been burned to death by Indians or ran off down South to mine for silver. No one at all was coming to ring the steeple bell or pray to this wooden, carved Jesus I was currently using to grind this whore's reanimated brain into the floorboards. I tossed it aside, reloaded, and filled Zoe with six more shots of lead. Even if she found the power within to get up off the floor and strike back at me, she would surely be able to use that wounded tit as a pencil. A saggy, bleeding pencil. Some books had been written with much less. I was sure of it.

What the skin walker formerly known as my wife had failed to realize was the fact that, apart from what you do and don't believe in, some places are just not meant for a showdown between the forces of good and evil. Just like the positive energy of the flowing water back at the Verde River, this here chapel flowed with goodness. To the creature who lay bleeding before me sent from the bowels of whatever Hades-like place that Indian bitch believed in, she was weakened once she entered the door. Like I said before, I had my own reservations when it came to religions and man-made belief systems, but you can't tell me for a second that some kind of all-powerful someone isn't looking over us out of mercy. If that were the case, I'd never have made it through the war with the Yankees, and I sure as Hell never would've made it this far in my weeklong battle with Zoe Telos. I wasn't worthy of this, you see. In my own mind, there was no way any type of god or goddess would grant me one smidgen of help to ward off the forces of evil on this particular night in this particular place. Then again, it's not for us, as people, to decide. We all think less of ourselves when it comes to looking inward. What we fail to realize is that it's never about how we view ourselves, but how others view us. That's why a mother will always love their children no matter how much bad they've done. I figured it was the same way when it came to an infinite being looking over all that he or she had created. Let's just say that I had a lot of time to think this through while I was knocked out and tied to a cross. I'm sure that Jesus man had the same epiphanies back in the day while dying in that desert sun as well. Why he chose to care about a single one of us human beings was beyond me, but it wasn't my puzzle to figure out. No one's ever written a whole book about me. At least not yet.

I looked down upon starving Zoe on the floor of the chapel. Bleeding her blackness all over the dirty floor once meant for the boots of soldiers and one guy pretending to be a dick doctor. I can't say much about the doctor because I didn't ever know him personally. Sure, doing what he did would indicate a certain amount of closeness, but I'm sure you understand what I'm trying to say. The soldiers, on the other hand, were something of which I knew volumes. I'd been fighting for my life since day one of this crazy world and today was, again, no different. I'd been taken as a baby when my parents were killed, forced to live on the streets in two of the meanest cities the United States had to offer, and then driven off to war for a cause I cared nothing about. We are born to fight, I guess. Straight from the cradle and into the grave, we battle for every breath we take. It's an allowance, really. Ultimately, you must earn them. Breaths, I mean. There were definitely no gifts of charity in the Arizona territory on this day, and what remained of my sweet wife fading at my feet would be no different. If she truly wanted to live past these next few precious moments, or at least what she'd call her own version of living, it was indeed going to take some convincing. I only had one bullet left between the ones I'd shot off and the ones that'd fell out of my gun belt while running like a fool between here and the rotting flesh of Poon down in the valley. Certainly, one last bullet to her head would be enough to do the trick in her current, weakened state.

"Well, well, well, old Zoe," I started up the last of our conversations while circling my former lover. "It would appear as though you've overestimated your powers in this place. You can thank two guys by the name of Liberman and Ravenwood if you meet them in the afterlife. They're either dead or rich silver miners by now, but it makes no never mind at this point. I never once imagined holy ground would be the leg up I needed to whip the likes of you and your Indian voodoo madness until I was pilfering through their belongings in the barracks. You must put all your faith in something. It doesn't matter who or what that is until the moment of need arrives. That Indian whore Hillary Hedgehog told me that I needed to make a choice when the time came, and I made it."

Zoe stared at me blankly as her chest heaved in labored fashion. Her breaths where getting farther and farther apart and it wasn't hard to see that she didn't have much life left in this world. I pointed the barrel of my Colt Army directly at her forehead to end both of our suffering. Hers? A quest for vengeance the likes of which can only be compared to that of a scorned mother at the end of her rope. In my absence, she'd made a life for herself and came to accept it for something normal. I have no idea who the man was that'd taken my place in her loneliness, but he was obviously enough to make her leave what she and I had together behind. They'd raised what an unknowing somebody would call a family and were making it all work just fine in the unforgiving desert of the Northern Arizona Territory. It was no place for anyone with any decency, really. Full of snakes, Indians, and other creatures that would rather kill you than get to know you. I'd left her all alone when I departed for war and, thinking back, well, I probably wouldn't have done anything differently if the roles were switched. I'd do whatever it took to move forward with life. Survive, so to speak. Sure enough, I came back home to put a burr in her saddle, and she didn't quite know how to make it all good again. Yes sir. That would make me want to give my life over to all that is horrible in this world and transform into some awful creature in an attempt to get back what

STARVING ZOE

was mine. After all, I took what was hers and tossed it down that dry well . . . but there was no point in crying over spilled baby milk at this point in the contest. I did what I did and there was no fixing it. Besides, it couldn't have been such a bad thing to do. I was standing upright in the House of God and she wasn't. That was all the reassurance I needed. Zoe's lips parted for the first time since she'd entered the entranceway to the church. I couldn't wait to hear the speech of wisdom she had planned for these tired ears.

Five words fell onto my soul like a hammer to an anvil. I flinched in sudden disgust and stumbled backward across the fallen, wooden carving of Jesus Christ I'd formerly been using as some type of battering ram on the face of my wife. Landing atop the blood covered floor of the sanctuary, I buried my face into my dirty hands and wept. I wept like a spoiled little girl with a skinned knee when pushed to the ground by a school yard bully. I, Robert Jack, was indeed that bully and began to wonder if those five words were the cue to stick the barrel of my revolver into my own mouth and swallow that final bullet for that sake of all that is wholesome in this world. She repeated the words again for good measure.

"Did you shoot our baby?"

Zoe wasn't exaggerating in the slightest. I didn't have much time to examine any details while I was blasting her into next week but be damned if she wasn't telling the truth. Her abdomen was protruding just like that Medicine Woman's posterior, except maybe a little lower than most people's lazy gut. Yes sir, there was definitely a baby 'something' squirming

🌵 137

around in there because I immediately noticed movement. I'm not quite sure how it was possible, the gestation period of skin walkers and all, but there it was right before my very eyes. Evil magic was still magic, I guessed, and this was indeed some evil magic brewing right in front of my face. Just then, Zoe further sealed my fate.

"It won't be long, you know," Zoe explained. "You'll be just like the two of us soon. You've been slowly changing since the moment you entered me in the pine forest, Robert. I know you've recognized the differences. One day at a time, one strange, stray thought after another, I know you could tell something was unusual. Your ability to heal at the river . . . "

I continued to sob uncontrollably as her near lifeless hands caressed her belly in the hopes I'd missed the mark. Glancing over out the corner of my eye, I reassured her that I didn't. I wasn't quite sure how. It wasn't like I'd been aiming much when I was letting her have it but somehow, someway, I'd shot her everywhere but the area in which she was so concerned. I grabbed Zoe by her trembling hand and placed it atop her abdomen for good measure. She smiled with the reassurance of my gesture and I knew in that moment the divine intervention and hints of the previous day had little to do with my victory over a foe. It had everything to do with my fate and future. I breathed a cleansing breath into the chilled, midnight air of the chapel as I laid my tired body down next to the remains of my wife. As gently as I possibly could, I maneuvered my left arm beneath her head for any type of comfort she'd still be willing to accept in her current state. If she was telling the honest truth, and I was responsible for my own healing at the river rather than the flowing water, then she'd be back on her feet soon.

"It's the only reason I refused to accept death on the banks of the river, Robert," she spoke to me softly with her final breaths. "I thought you were dead, so I moved on. All I wanted to do was give us a chance to have the type of life we were robbed of by the hands of fate. It was the only way I knew how. The last choice. The only choice that mattered."

Make the right choice, Robert Jack. Make the right choice. It was at that point when the words of Hillary Hedgehog, the Indian Medicine Woman, made sense to me. I'd left Zoe Telos for dead on the banks of the Verde River and, no matter how much power the old crone had in her, there wasn't enough to save my wife's life. There was only enough to transform it into something, never mind how hideous, that could carry on. A vessel. Granted, those Navajo bitches have a twisted way of doing the unthinkable, but she shuffled the cards and pulled skin walker from the deck. That's why she chose not to kill me during our encounters. That's why she forced me into sex in the pine forests of the mountains. That's why I was still alive at this moment laying in puddles of blood along the chapel floorboards as it poured from the wounds of the woman I loved. Who was I to say what 'living' truly was? It was different for everyone no matter how it was viewed by others. For some, it was worshipping a book with strange symbols that you kept hidden in the very bottom of your footlocker. For others, it was a silver trinket you held onto for dear life in times of need. Me? I chose to be in love with a dying skin walker on the floor of an abandoned church with some freak of a half breed child on the way. I did the only sensible thing that accompanied a realization such as that. I placed my revolver with the last remaining bullet into my own mouth and pulled the trigger for the sake of sanity. In my fading seconds, I again witnessed the silhouette of the Indian Medicine Woman in the church doorway.

"It is finished," she spoke with a certain amount of surety.

It was indeed.

Perhaps you've heard my cautionary tale of woe as a whisper on the wind in a severe time of need. Maybe it's come to you in your sleep as a nightmarish portend of what's approaching in your own life if you choose not to do what's right and wholesome during an encounter at the crossroads. Just like I said in the beginning, forgiveness is overrated. Death is final. Revenge, however, dances between the fine lines of mortality and eternity. Love always finds a way. Seven days later, in its own cryptic fashion, it did.

Cursed from birth. Cured by death. I was home.

THE END

ACKNOWLEDGEMENTS

A very special 'Thank You' to my beta readers:

Samantha Cloud-Miller
Cristi Lane Williams
Tanya Rhodes Reynolds
Kimberley Kizziar
Dan Carson

ABOUT THE AUTHOR

C. Derick Miller is a dark fiction author, Gonzo journalist, screenwriter, poet, ordained minister, and ASCAP songwriter born in the town of Greenville, Texas. His influences include Hunter S. Thompson, Kevin Smith, Shawn Mullins, and Del James. Currently the Senior Writer/Junior Producer for AtuA Productions, he resides in the Bishop Arts District of Dallas, Texas where he has a price on his head for his short story "Hell Paso" contained in the #1 bestselling Death's Head Press anthology *And Hell Followed*. He wishes he were making up that last part but . . . it is nice to be wanted.